Captain G.E.M. and the Green Coats

The Stowaway

By

Justin Kennon

Cover Designed by

Rosso Winch

Chapter 1

It was supposed to be a peaceful cruise for the people aboard the A. S. Leonardo. It was the top-of-the-line vessel in the entire Valen Kingdom. The Leonardo had the finest food, the richest music, and the cream of high societies crop in the ballroom. If some moron did try to cause trouble, they would have to deal with some of the best trained soldiers in the entire Kingdom.

It's just too bad that "moron" had just shown up, currently fighting with the last of the guards near the only exit for them to escape from.

He was tall, with messy blue hair. His green eyes and big smile showed off his confidence and cockiness. He wore no shirt, but his muscular chest made it clear he did not need one. His green jacket hung around his neck like a cape. On it was the symbol of his crew, the letter G circling the letter C, the symbol of the Green Coats pirates. His pants were as black as the deepest, darkest hole, where no light could escape. His shoes were a fine pair, made for any occasion. In each hand were his Elgin

1

Cutlass Revolvers; "S2BU" in his left, and "URF'D" in his right.

The guard was wielding a spear that he jabbed at the moron, who dodged and spun as he laughed. The guard's eyes stared daggers at his enemy as sharp as the point on his spear from under his helmet and he used his entire armor-clad body to attack.

The guard thrust the spear for the Green Coat's heart but was stopped by the two cutlasses catching the spear and forcing it upwards. The Green Coat barely dodged the strike by kneeling and bending backwards, getting two or three strands of hair cut off.

As the guard continued to push forwards, unable to stop his momentum, the Green Coat quickly got back to his feet, and used one leg to kick the guard back in the gut.

The guard stumbled back but was in no pain. He took a moment too look down and hold his stomach, but that would be his undoing. As he looked back up, the pirate was charging forward, not giving the guard any time to mount a counterattack as he jumped into the air.

All the guard could do was lean back, as the pirate flipped forwarded and placed the tips of his weapons right under the guard's eyes, doing a perfect handstand right on top of him.

It only lasted for a second, but that was the last second of the guard's life. The last thing he would see in this world were the barrels of cutlass pistols, as they went off.

With the last guard dead, the pirate fell with the body falling to its back and flipped back to his feet onto a table. He took a moment, before turning to the patrons of the ship staring in fear and pressed against the wall. Above them stood painted glass works of kings, heroes, and religious figures. Soldier bodies lay dead around the room with bullet holes, cuts, and stabs covering them. But the most frightening sight to all the passengers was the body of a soldier that had both his eyes shot out of his skull with two cuts right below the bullet holes, just like their last hope.

"Ladies and Gentlemen!" He addressed the crowd, "I am Captain G.E.M. of the Green Coats, and we're here to rob you blind."

"But we can see you!" someone in the crowd shouted.

G.E.M. lowered his arms and head, frowning, before turning his gun towards the man that called out to him. Not even looking his way, he shot the man right between the eyes, dead.

"Did anyone see that?" he asked the crowd, glaring at them. They all shook their heads.

"Good." He jumped off the table, performing a front flip. "Now," he pulled an entire tablecloth off, turning it into a holding bag, "before I was so rudely interrupted; we are here to rob you blind. So please give us all your money, jewelry, clothes... On second thought... Keep your clothes on." With that, he touched a communicator on his ear. "How are we doing, Sunshine?"

"We're looking good, Captain." A blond guy wearing his own green jacket replied over the communicator with his fingers typing away at his keyboard. "I've blocked all the calls for help and cracked the security five minutes ago."

"Thanks, Sunshine." G.E.M. told him, before switching to another channel. "How's it going with those supplies, Pinky?"

"It's going well, Captain!" Pinky shouted over the sounds of gunfire. She was in her early twenties with pink hair going down to her neck. She wore the Green Coat's iconic jacket over a black shirt with short brown jeans and sneakers. "Alan and Bob are taking their sweet time however!" She quickly hid behind a cargo box she was using for cover as bullets whizzed over her head. Wondering what was taking them so long, she could see light coming from the open storage room door.

In the room two young men around the same age as Pinky were arguing.

"Man," Alan told his twin brother as they picked up another chest, "the chest is heavy." It was easy to tell them apart as Alan had shaved the left side of his head and Bob had only shaved the right.

Other than that, they wore the same jacket with red shirts, blue jean pants, and boots.

"Of course, it's heavy!" Bob shouted over the gun fire right outside. "It's full of gold!"

"It's heavy but not gold heavy," Alan said.

"Look," Bob told him, "what are chests full of? Gold and jewels. Gold and jewels are heavy. Ergo, chests are heavy."

"Yeah… but…" Alan started, before he was interrupted.

"Get the lead out you two!" Pinky shouted.

"It's a chest!" they both shouted back at her.

"I don't care!" Pinky kept shouting while continuing the firefight against the guards. "I can't hold these guards back forever."

"Okay, we're coming." Bob told her as he and Alan heading into the fray.

Alan carried the bulk of the chest out into the hall, while Bob fired at the guards. "You would think they'd just give up by now," Bob shouted to no one in particular.

"Where's our back up?" Pinky shouted into her headset, as she started to get pinned down by the two remaining guards.

Behind the guards a man in the shadows lifted his weapon, a bladed-edge boomerang over his head, and tossed it with immense force.

One guard didn't see it coming behind him, as the weapon decapitated his head. The head rolled across to the ground next to the other guard.

Pinky panicked for a moment before ducking underneath the swirling blade.

The other guard was next to the now body-less head, turning his gun on the object that was coming right at him.

He fired at the flying object. The bullet hit it, causing it to fall to the floor. Because all the focus was on the boomerang that was coming after him at the time, he failed to pay attention to Pinky shooting him right in the face.

As the body fell, Pinky turned her attention towards the one that threw the boomerang. "Thanks, Boomer."

Boomer slowly walked over to her, revealing himself out of the shadows. His entire head was covered by a mask designed to look like a compass. Each glove had a letter on it to show east and west, and his pants had the letters for north and south on his knees. The left side of his skin-tight shirt had the Green Coats' symbol displayed.

"Is everything okay?" Pinky asked with the adrenaline from the shootout slowly starting to wear off.

Boomer just nodded, walking past the bodies, and picking up his boomerang.

"Hey, Pinky!" Bob called out to her, "We got the entire lot on the ship."

"Including the strangely heavy one!" Alan jumped into the conversation, but that just started another argument with Bob.

Pinky ignored them as she contacted G.E.M. "Did you hear that Captain?"

"Yes, Pinky, thank you." he replied, tossing the tablecloth full of valuables over his shoulder. He stood under a painted glass work that showed a man in a loincloth, his wrists and ankles tied with rope, making the man form a Y shape.

"And so," he bowed to the partiers, "I bid you farewell."

"You won't get away with this," someone spoke up. "You won't make it to your ship with all the doors locked."

"Who said anything about doors?" G.E.M. smirked, tapping his communicator. "Sunshine, a little help if you please."

"Yes, Captain!" Sunshine answered, pressing a button.

Ten seconds later, a grappling hook shattered through the painted window. G.E.M. grabbed the rope, stepped on the hook, and with a quick tug was pulled out with the loot.

The passengers were all in shock, rushing towards the window. There they saw the Green Coats' ship, the Green-Eyed Monster, flying into the wild blue yonder.

It was a large, all green airship. Its underbelly was completely flat except for a turret gun that hung below and an access area where the grappling hook holding G.E.M. was dangling from. There were four wings total on the ship, with two large wings located at the end close to the rockets and two small wings near the front. At the top, which the passengers could not see, was another turret gun and the tail.

The high winds blew around G.E.M. and his spoils as the green airship over his head carried them away from the luxury airship his Green Coats had just robbed.

A large grin grew on his face, as G.E.M. saw the passengers from the cruise ship, only able to watch as he was lifted into his ship and blasted off.

Miles away from the ship, the cargo doors closed under his feet, G.E.M. stepped down from the grappling hook to the cargo bay floor, and he greeted most of his crew.

Pinky, Alan, Bob, and Boomer had packed all the crates, chests, and other goodies they were able to steal around them. With them was a young woman with black hair tied in a ponytail, wearing a long skirt, long-sleeved shirt, and an apron. She was clearly the cook of their ship by her clothing.

The metal-grey cargo hold was wide enough to hold their spoils and allow them to walk around if need be. The hallway connecting the hold with the rest of the ship went straight through the vessel, as a couple lights shined out from the other rooms.

"Good job today crew!" He told them. "Tonight, we feast!"

The crew cheered, with Bob and Alan high fiving each other. Boomer just quietly clapped his hands, as Pinky and the other woman smiled with excitement.

"I can't wait to see what we have to cook with." The woman stated.

"I'm sure anything you make will be delicious May." G.E.M. addressed her with a smiled. "But first, look at the loot I got from those walking piggy banks." He dropped the bag, and it spilled onto the floor, causing wallets, money, and jewels to fall at their feet.

They stared a bit in awe, but quickly returned their attention to their captain.

"By the way," he asked, "Where's Sunshine? Victor? And…" He paused, feeling a cold, small shiver rises up his spine. "April?"

"Sunshine is currently piloting the ship." Pinky explained. "He's having Victor and April help with making sure we getaway clean."

"Good…" G.E.M. sighed but getting straightened out. "All right! How about we start opening these up and see what kind of booty we got!"

"I think we should open that weirdly overweight chest." Alan pointed over at the chest, before Bob smacked him aside the head.

"Shut up." Bob told them, getting his head smacked by Alan.

The two were about ready to start a fight, but Pinky was able to get them in line by threatening, "If you two damage anything in here!

I'm going to blow your empty heads clean off your shoulders!"

While that was going on, May was looking over the crates. "I wonder which of these has the food in them."

Boomer just stood there, watching his crew members, when he thought he saw the lid on the chest Alan had first pointed to open a bit. It was only a second before the lid quickly shut.

G.E.M. was trying to keep everyone in line, as Boomer tapped him on the shoulder to get his attention.

"Hm, what is it Boomer?" G.E.M. asked him.

Boomer pointed over at the chest before putting his hands together at the thumbs and index fingers, with the palms facing out. He lifted them up slightly, while separating them apart.

G.E.M. knew Boomer was telling him to open that chest first. "Okay." He nodded, getting serious.

The rest of the crew stopped what they were doing, as G.E.M. made his way over to the chest, slowly kneeling and taking the lid in his hands.

The rest of them gathered behind him, watching as the lid was thrown open with a quick flick.

The entire crew were shocked, as it was not gold, or jewels, or anything of that like, but a little girl dressed in a beautiful, elegant dress staring back at them with terror in her eyes.

Chapter 2

"Oh, shit," G.E.M. cursed as he stared at the elegant girl that laid in the chest.

She had to be no older than eight, ten tops. Her golden blond hair was perfectly made into a bun. Her clothing was a clear indication that she was from a noble house and not just some worker girl. Her skin and clothing were slightly filthy, but that was from hiding in the chest.

The crew saw the look of terror on her face, which was obvious when it came to coming face to face with the Green-Eyed Monster himself.

G.E.M. continued cursing in anger, seeming to stomp around where he stood. He looked like an overgrown child in front of his crew and the child in the chest.

In his anger, G.E.M. pulled out his cutlass-pistol, pointing the barrel right between the girl's eyes, and the end of the blade on the tip her nose.

"Name!" he demanded, pulling the hammer back. "Now!" It was clear that he was going to shoot her right then and there if she did not answer.

The little girl stuttered for a bit as G.E.M. slowly started pulling the trigger. "Pr-Princess Zephyrus!" she shouted at the top of her lungs in fear.

G.E.M. was shocked, loosening his trigger finger, and putting the pistol back into its holster. He turned around, walking past his crew to calm down.

They noticed a twitching in his eye, and his mouth hung slightly open.

"Wait!" Pinky spoke up, looking back at the girl. "You're Princess Zephyrus? THE Princess Zephyrus? Royal Heiress of the Astuio throne? The same Astuio family that rules the flying country of Valen? One of the seven Kingdoms of the skies?"

Alan looked over at his brother, smacking him aside the head. "See! I told you it wasn't full of gold!"

Bob growled, thinking of all the ways he was going to hurt Alan when he got the chance.

Princess Zephyrus looked over at Pinky, nodding in respond. "Can I please get out of this chest?"

Pinky looked over at G.E.M. still arguing and fusing with himself, so she answered for him. "Sure."

"Thank you." Zephyrus told her, bowing her head out of respect. She stepped out of the chest, allowing the crew to see her entire dress. The patterns on it were gorgeous, golden fabric flowing from an upside-down triangle right over her heart like waves. Inside the triangle was a man in what they could guess was a white robe in a Y pose, with his head hanging down to hide his face.

The dress around her legs was slick and smooth, reaching to the floor. The sleeves were long, reaching down to her wrists.

"Oh my gosh!" May squealed, "A real live Princess! This is so exciting! Can we keep her?"

Boomer stared at the Princess, seeming to study her, wondering how this was going to play out.

"Void No!" G.E.M. shouted at his crew in a panic. He looked back over at said princess and walked back over to her in a calm manner. Crossing his arms over his chest, he looked down at her with a dark glare. "What were you doing hiding in that chest?" he questioned her, "And for that matter, what the hell were you doing down there anyway? Wouldn't a Princess like you be in some private room, with security guards? I'm going to have to tell Sunshine he screwed up."

"No one knew I was on the ship." Princess Zephyrus responded, getting everyone's attention yet again, including the demonic green eyes of G.E.M. waiting for her to continue.

"Well…" Zephyrus started to explain before G.E.M. pulled out his gun and put it back in her face.

"Before you start talking again," G.E.M. warned her, "if you're lying, I'll fill you full of holes."

Princess Zephyrus gulped, fearing G.E.M. would just shoot her anyway before hearing her story.

"My Grandfather, King Xenos, has been ill and bed-ridden for a few months when he heard that his adviser, Yves, was going to betray him in a coup."

"I think I remember hearing the king was ill." Pinky spoke up, cupping her chin as she tried to remember.

"That's horrible!" May interrupted, placing her hands over her mouth in shock.

"May, Pinky," G.E.M. addressed them, "Please, it's rude to interrupt someone when their talking."

"Oh, sorry." May apologized, backing off.

"Sorry Captain." Pinky respectfully apologized, slightly bowing her head.

G.E.M. turned his attention back to Princess Zephyrus. "How did your grandfather find out about this coup?" G.E.M. asked.

"There were those still loyal to my grandfather, and he advised them to get me out of the country." Zephyrus answered, "but because of his illness, he had to stay behind."

"That's… understandable." G.E.M. said, seeming to have thought it over and it was would be believable.

"And they hid you in the chest and placed you on the ship to get you out before the attack started?" Pinky finished her story. Zephyrus nodded at her words, before G.E.M. could say anything to Pinky.

"That's a weird one." Alan interrupted next, but quietly shut it when Bob slapped him behind the head.

"I was supposed to be heading to our allies in Hǔ Bǎi Hé, but…" Zephyr started to say.

"But we attacked the ship, and 'kidnapped' you." G.E.M. interrupted next, finishing what she was about to say.

"I thought you were Yves' forces, having learned about my escape," Zephyrus told them.

"But now seeing you're not them, what do you plan to do to me?"

They all looked at her, then at each other, then back to her. G.E.M. cupped his chin, thinking of the options. "We could… possibly help you get to Hŭ Băi Hé," G.E.M. suggested, raising Princess Zephyrus's hopes. "But we're going to need to get some help, and it would be a lot of work. And honestly, I really don't want to ask for *their* help, nor do all that work."

That crushed Princess Zephyrus's hopes, but it was too much to ask a pirate to help her.

"But we could see about handing you over to this Yves guy." G.E.M. thought aloud, rubbing the back of his head. "I mean, you Valens kind of deserve it. And if we hand you over, we might get a nice reward out of it."

Zephyrus switched back to being terrified, after she heard him suggest that.

"Although…" He started to suggest, before Princess Zephyrus interrupted him.

"What if I pay you?" Princess Zephyrus suggested out of fear.

G.E.M. pulled out his cutlass-pistol once again, aiming it at her. "Don't interrupt me either." He told her.

"Sorry." She coward back, trying to shrink herself.

"As I was saying," G.E.M. continued, twirling his weapon, before holstering it. "It would just be easier to throw you right into the endless Void, and not have to deal with you ever again." G.E.M. smirked, liking that idea the most.

Zephyrus and the other Green Coats looked on with fright about his idea.

"But I don't want to be responsible for killing a child." He said, changing his expression once again.

"What if I pay you?" Princess Zephyrus repeated her proposal.

G.E.M. looked down at Princess Zephyrus when she blurted it out. "And how do you propose you'll do that? You are all alone. You just possibly lost your Kingdom. And… we hate Valen.

"Once I get my Kingdom back," Princess Zephyrus explained, collecting all the courage she could find inside herself. "I will reward a king's ransom."

G.E.M. laughed, finding her last choice of words comical.

"I could even do anything you want." She continued, trying to ignore his laugher. "I know there is something you Green Coats have wanted from Valen as long as you've been pirates. I can pardon you of your greatest crime!"

G.E.M. and the other Green Coats gasped, shocked at such an offer. G.E.M. looked at his crew for a moment, then told the Princess. "Give us a moment." He walked over to his crew, and they circled around to talk.

Princess Zephyrus thought that she would be alright at that moment. Knowing there was no way they would deny the chance of a lifetime.

The Green Coats seem to have finished their talk, as G.E.M. walked back to her, quickly grabbing her by the arm.

The others watched as their captain dragged the princess down the ship's hallway.

"Let me go!" The Princess demanded, as G.E.M. dragged her down the hall. She tried scratching at his hand to loosen his grip, but this only made G.E.M. tighten. "My offer is one of a kind."

Reaching a door in the middle of the hall, G.E.M. opened it to reveal a small bathroom, before tossing the princess inside.

Falling to the floor Princess Zephyrus looked over at G.E.M. "What's the big idea?" She asked him.

"We need to talk it over with the whole crew." He replied, "Now you stay here, while we decide what to do with you." With that, he shut the door right in her face, locking it from his side so she couldn't get out.

Chapter 3

The princess pounded on the door, demanding she be let out, but G.E.M. ignored her, walking away.

As he walked off, Pinky came up beside him. "Please tell me you were not serious about all those things you said!" she told her captain. "I could see handing her back to her Kingdom, but killing her? Throwing her into the Void?"

"I said I'd do it if she was lying," he told her, not looking her way. "I did promise to get her to Hǔ Bǎi Hé if she was telling the truth. We'd just have to hand her over to the Zǐ Sè Dēng Pào. They have ties to the Hǔ Bǎi Hé government."

Pinky nodded, understanding her captain's decision on giving the Princess to the Zǐ Sè Dēng Pào to escort her. "If there is anyone that can get the princess safely into Hǔ Bǎi Hé, it's them."

"That's only if she is telling the truth," G.E.M. pointed out to her as they entered the bridge.

The door opened, showing a pathway with two sets of stairs going down to a lower level on each side. The pathway led to a rotating armchair that was clearly for the captain, wide enough for just one person to walk across. The lower level had four seats.

Two seats faced forward, facing out the window, as well as at several screens that allowed them to see a few blind spots. In the pilot seat, Sunshine held tight to the controls, steering smoothly through the blue skies.

The copilot was a middle-age man with salt and pepper hair. He didn't wear the recognizable coat of the crew, but a flannel shirt, blue overalls, and steel toe work boots. Around his waist was a tool belt that held a hammer, wrench, screwdriver, and other tools a mechanic would need.

On the right side was a currently empty seat that looked over a screen that monitored the weather readings in the area.

One seat faced the left wall that had a radar screen being watched by a woman that looked like

May, but a few years older, scanning for possible ships and enemies. Her glasses hung on her face, with a rope going around it to keep it from falling to the floor if it ever came off, and her hair was in a bun as well. She wore a doctor's coat, but it was green instead of white, and it had the Green Coats symbol on the left chest. Under the coat was a casual navy-blue dress with the skirt stopping at her knees, ending with flat, slip-on shoes. She looked over at G.E.M. "Welcome back Captain." She greeted, giving a sly, seductive smile.

"No time April." G.E.M. told her, while walking over to his chair. Above the windshield was a flat screen.

Pinky headed down the stairs to the lower section.

"Sunshine," G.E.M. called his name, as he sat in his chair. "You got some explaining to do."

Sunshine turned to look at his captain, as Pinky went over to take his place. "What's wrong?"

G.E.M. didn't say anything, looking over at Pinky to speak. "Your checking of the guest list was incomplete. We ended up getting a stowaway."

"What?" Sunshine shouted in shock. "There is no way I messed up! I triple checked the guest list, passenger list, and crew."

"She said she was smuggled onto the ship, but now she's our problem," G.E.M. explained, "And she's a big problem."

"What are you talking about Captain?" Sunshine asked.

G.E.M. looked over at the middle-aged mechanic. "Victor, you are relieved of your duty here. You can go and get some rest, or something to eat."

Victor got out of the copilot seat and addressed his captain. "Thanks Captain, I'll go check on the engines, make sure they are in working order." With that, Victor headed off the bridge.

G.E.M. turned his attention back to Sunshine. "I need you to look into any reports from

Valen. Look up anything you can find dealing with Princess Zephyrus, King Xenos, and Yves."

"Why do you want me to look up the royal Valen family?" Sunshine asked.

"Just do it." G.E.M. demanded, as Sunshine sat down. "See if you can find anything about a coup."

Sunshine rapidly typed away at his keyboard, quickly finding something for all of them to see. "No news about any coup, Captain," Sunshine told him, "But I have learned that King Xenos is dead."

"Dead?" G.E.M. repeated.

"It appears he was found dead in his bed this morning," Sunshine explained, pulling an article up on the main screen for them all to see. "There's no word about foul play, but they are considering all possibilities."

"Maybe this is the coup Zephyrus spoke of," Pinky suggested, looking over at G.E.M. "If they do not know what killed the king, they could blame anyone or anything they want."

"Including us if they learn we have the Princess," G.E.M. pointed out to them. "Sunshine, what can you find on this Yves?"

"Give me a minute," Sunshine told him, punching away at the keyboard at a blinding rate. "I got it." He pulled up a picture of a massively tall man in about his thirties. The picture showed him in royal attire with metals all over his chest. His hair was long, reaching down his mid-back, with the left side of his hair being pure bleach blond, and the right side was blacker than a starless night. Upon his back was a massive sword that was not in any scabbard, but the blade stood out for all to see.

"It says here he was born to a single mother with no record of who the father is," Sunshine read up on Yves. "Holy cow! He's over 7 feet tall!"

Everyone on the bridge snapped their heads over to look at him in complete shock. "There's no way!" Pinky shouted.

"It's real," Sunshine told them, pulling up a photo of Yves standing next to a statue of a man holding an open book and a feather pen, which showed them at about equal high. "That's called the Recorder, after a Romek god that looks over the world and records everything that happens. It was made by Olivier Poulin and stands at seven feet exact."

"Damn!" G.E.M. cursed, "He is massive! What's that sword on his back?" He pointed at Yves' weapon.

"That's the…" Sunshine drew out, as he searched. "Dragger another Romek god, but of the dead this time, that would drag the souls of the damned and those that tried to escape it down to face their judgement."

"Got to admit, the guy sure knows how to name his blade," G.E.M. admired.

"There is also a news feed that has just gone out from Yves about the King's death," Sunshine announced, throwing it up on the main screen, and playing it as Yves starting his speech.

"My fellow countrymen of Valen," Yves addressed them, clearly talking to the people of

Valen. "It saddens me to say that King Xenos was found dead this morning in his bed."

The entire audience gasped at the news of their King's passing.

"A servant found the King laying in his bed not breathing, when bringing him his breakfast." Yves continued to explain to the crowd. "Due to the King's failing health and age, the servant walked into his room. When she got no response from him, she thought he was still sleeping and went over to wake him. She softly pulled the covers off and tried to wake him. When she could not wake him, she started to worry and checked his pulse."

"How did the King die?" A patron from the crowd shouted out to him.

"We do not know at this time, but we are looking into it." Yves answered them. "We are hoping that God peacefully took the King in the night."

"Where is the Princess?" a reporter asked him.

Yves glared over at him. "I am told she is currently on a cruise ship." Yves addressed him, "We are currently trying to contact them."

"What will happen now that the King is dead?" another reporter asked him.

"The Princess is still too young to take the throne at this time," Yves explained. "As such, the royal court will handle all issues of the Kingdom till Princess Zephyrus comes of age. If you excuse me, I need to get back to my duties and make sure the Kingdom is stable."

The video ended, with GEM, Pinky, April and Sunshine looking at each other. "Boss?" Sunshine asked him. "Does this stowaway happen to be a little girl?"

G.E.M. sighed, cracking an unhappy smile at Sunshine. "Yeah Sunshine. We accidently kidnapped Princess Zephyrus."

"How in the world did you do it Captain?" April asked him, either out of confusion, fear, or admiration.

"She was hiding in one of the chests in the cargo bay, okay?" G.E.M. shot up from his seat, speaking loudly. "How long ago was that new report broadcasted?"

Sunshine quickly turned back, checking the timestamp. "About two hours."

"Pinky!" He shouted out to his first mate. "Get us out of here…"

Before he could finish, alarms started to go off, and lights flashing.

April turned back to the radar screen. "We have several Valen warships coming our way!"

"Crap!" G.E.M. cursed. "We need to get out of here." He pressed a button on his chair, opening the ships speakers. "Boomer! We need you on the bridge right away!"

"I'll try to get us in the clouds!" Pinky shouted, steering the ship.

"I'll start working on jamming their radar!" Sunshine added, punching away at his keyboard.

G.E.M. sat back in his chair, gripping the arms. "It's too bad the gods are not real. Cause we could really use their help right now."

Chapter 4

The Green-Eyed Monster carefully moved within a massive cloud, as a Valen patrol ship was flying by them.

G.E.M. and his crew watching with nervous anticipation, as the gargantuan ship slowly flew by. It's pearl-white hull made the sun's rays reflect off like a mirror, bronze side cannons seeming to aim right at them. Ready to fire if they moved even a single inch out of their cloud cover. The cannons on top of the ship were three times larger than the side cannons, with enough power to rip the Green-Eyed Monster in two with a single blast.

"How are we doing hiding from their sensors?" G.E.M. asked, while they listened to the radar screen.

"They don't seem to notice us Captain." April said, carefully watching the radar screen herself.

"Let's just hope it stays that way." G.E.M. said, glancing his eyes over to Sunshine for a second. Sunshine was the best hacker in all the skies, but G.E.M. could not help but feel the sweat building in his pores from the sight of the Valen ship.

"We're completely hidden from their radar." Sunshine answered, typing away at his keyboard, making every stroke count like the notes in a musical performance. "All we can hope for now is that they don't accidentally run into us."

"What about the data the ship currently has on them?" G.E.M. questioned his hacker some more.

"I'm collecting all that I can." He explained. "Looking for anything that mentions the King, the Princess, Yves, the Leonardo, or us."

The tension on the bridge was thick. Everyone could feel the pressure and fear from the sight of the Valen ship squeezing around their necks like two massive hands coming from behind them. It was a miracle they did not slip up.

"Alright," G.E.M. nodded, slowly getting out of his seat while shaking. "Pinky. Keep the ship moving with the clouds till they are far away from us. I don't want us getting caught in a fire fight with this many Valen ships. I'm going to make sure the rest of the crew is not doing anything stupid."

"You mean Alan and Bob." Pinky looked over at him. It was a normal joke, but there was a worried expression on her face.

"Yeah," G.E.M. assured her, "and our 'guest'. Boomer," he addressed his navigator. "Continued helping them with navigating with the cloud."

Boomer looked over from his station, giving G.E.M. a thumbs up.

"Sunshine," He called out to him next. "Keep up the work. I want us to see home again soon."

"Okay Captain. We got this." Sunshine replied, as G.E.M. headed off the bridge.

Once G.E.M. was off the bridge and the door closed behind him, he let out the breath he was holding in a reliving sigh. He was used to navigating passed Valen's airships thanks to Boomer's navigation, Sunshine's hacking, and his time flying around the area as well, but those Valen warships always scared the Void out of him whenever he saw them.

He had fought, and beat a few before, but those were in unfair fights where he and his crew attacked by surprise. And even then, they would quickly cut out their communication, board the ship, and take the fight right up in their faces.

"It is going to be okay." G.E.M. told himself, "Sunshine will keep us safe and Boomer will know which way to go." Feeling convinced by his own words, G.E.M. continued down the hall feeling confident again.

G.E.M. found Alan and Bob guarding the restroom, playing cards, without a care in the world about being hunted by Valen's airships, or the fact that the princess was calling out to them from the other side of the door.

It seems they were playing Kingdoms. It's a simple card game; the goal is to have the most of whatever suit is the "resource" they are fighting over and leave their opponents with nothing. The

Ten of Swords was lying next to the deck of cards, showing the resource they were fighting over.

Alan seemed to have his brother beat in all resources of the game, with more Hearts, Clubs, Diamonds, and Swords. But Bob wasn't far behind, and he had most of the Royal Families on his side with the two Kings, three Queens, and one Jack.

"I want out of here!" Princess Zephyrus yelled from the top of her lungs, banging on the door.

"How's it going?" He asked them, ignoring the princess' demands to be freed.

"It's close." Alan told him.

"Well, finish up fast. We might need you two in the turret guns soon." He told them, before noticing May walked up to them with some exotic foods.

"Getting food ready for the annual 'successful plundering'?" He asked her.

"Oh yes Captain!" She smiled excitedly, "I got so many ideas going through my head for new dishes."

"Well... you better wait on that." G.E.M. told her, "At least until we escape the Valens."

"You mean we're not going to have a party?" Bob asked G.E.M.

"But we always have a party after a plunder." Alan pointed out.

"I didn't say we were not going to have one." G.E.M. told them, holding his hands out in hopes to calm them. "It's just on a short hold till we're in safer skies and know what to do about the Princess."

"I demand you let me go!" The princess shouted, but no one paid attention. "It smells in here!"

"But she already explained what was going on, and she needs our help to get to Hǔ Bǎi Hé." April said.

"Yeah, but we don't know how those Valen ships are going to react to us, if they learn she's here on the ship." G.E.M. said to her.

"Why not use her as a hostage?" Bob suggested out of the blue.

"But what if-" May started to explain, before an explosion rocked the ship, causing G.E.M., May, and the brothers to crash into the side of their ship. The food in May's arms went flying, causing them to break and make a mess. Sirens rang throughout the ship, red light filling the halls.

"Captain!" Sunshine should over the speakers. "You got to get to the bridge, right away!"

"Get to your areas!" G.E.M. shouted and wasted no time, pushing past May and the twins.

Everyone rushed to their respective position. May went to a safe area, while Bob and Alan raced to their turrets. More explosions rattled the ship, as he was thrown between the walls.

G.E.M. was finally able to get to the bridge, rubbing his sore left shoulder from the pain that was running through it, as well as his entire body. "What the Void is happening?" G.E.M shouted at his crew, before seeing a Valen air ship right in front of him.

"What the hell!" G.E.M. shouted at Sunshine, "I thought you said we were hidden from their radar!"

"I don't know how they found us!" Sunshine shouted, punching away at his keyboard in a mad dash.

G.E.M. growled under his breath, as more explosions happened around them, throwing he to the floor. Everyone else had buckled into their seats to keep them from being thrown all over the place.

The pain was aching all over his body, crawling on the floor to his seat and holding tight to the pathway so not to be sent flying again.

Another explosion rocked the ship, as G.E.M. finally got in his seat. He buckled himself in, as he noticed that someone was trying to contact him by a light flashing on his left armrest.

He pressed it, and a two-way video chat screen came up, showing the captain of the other ship. The captain was well dressed, wearing a full button-up suit, which had a dozen medals over his left chest. He seemed to be in his late 40s to early 50s, from the facial hair he was showing. It had a few grey hairs in it, proving his age.

The symbol of Valen showed on the hat that covered his hair and his right chest. An upside triangle showing a man in the center doing a Y post.

"How dare you G.E.M!" The Valen captain snarled at him, "How dare you and your Green Coats attack the Leonardo!"

'How did they find out so fast?' G.E.M. thought, as he addressed the other captain.

"We've attacked your fancy ass ships before, how is this any different?"

"Don't hide it you green devils!" The captain shouted. "You did a thousand despicable things during your reign of terror, but destroying the cruise ship the Princess was on; killing her in the process, is the highest sin you have committed since you were born."

"Just what the Void are you talking about!" G.E.M. shouted back, getting pissed off at the other captain.

"Don't play stupid with me!" The captain stated. "You sky demons are the ones that blew the

Leonardo out of the skies and murdered Princess
Zephyrus!"

Chapter 5

"What in god's name are you talking about?" G.E.M. asked him, finding the news unbelievable; because the news was false. His mouth started to open to tell them they had the princess alive and well, locked up inside their restroom, but the Captain spoke first.

"We got a distress call a while back." The Captain told him, pressing down on a button.

"Please help!" A static voice shouted over the speakers. "We're under attack by the Green Coat Pirates!"

Hearing that S.O.S. over their speakers, G.E.M. looked over at Sunshine; getting the same unbelievable look he was giving.

"There's no way that call got out." Sunshine insured him, "I'm the best there is. I made sure to hack and blocked their communications." G.E.M. turned his head back to the Captain on the screen.

"When he got there," The Captain started speaking again. "All we found was THIS!" He shouted, as a picture of a devastated Leonardo appeared on the screen

Sunshine's mouth hung open and his eyes bugged out, Pinky covered her mouth with her hands, Boomer could not have any expression on his face, and G.E.M. just stared directly at the picture.

There, before them, was the Leonardo. From port to starboard, blast marks covered the ship. Smoke rose out of some of the holes and out of the top. It could barely stay up, leaning over toward it tail end. Closer examination showed the passengers on the ship were dead.

G.E.M. could see some of the upper-class members he stole from earlier that day. All of them were lying lifeless on the floor, in chairs, or over tables. They all had bullet and stab wounds all over their bodies.

"Not a single survivor was found." The Captain told them off screen.

He started to shake, balling up his fist. "My crew did not destroy that ship!" G.E.M. shouted, shooting up from his chair. With a swift wave of his arm, he continued to proclaim, "Yes! My crew and I did attack the Leonardo, but we left all the passengers on that ship alive! Say for a few soldiers." He whispered the last part under his breath. "And-"

"We've been ordered to fire on sight!" The Captain shouted back, "And to make sure there are no survivors! Just like you did to the Leonardo."

"There's no way those pictures are real! We didn't kill all those people!" G.E.M. shouted, slamming his fists on the chair's arms.

"They are!" The Captain shouted back with just as much rage. "And we've been given orders to kill you and your crew on sight! OPEN FIRE!" The bombardment started up again, as the screen was cut out.

"Alan! Bob!" G.E.M. shouted over the speakers, "Fire! Sunshine! Get us back in contact with the main ship! We need to tell them the Princess is alive!"

"I'm trying Captain!" He shouted over the explosions, "But they are kicking me out every time I get my foot through the door!" Another explosion rocked the ship, causing Sunshine's hands to slip on the keyboard. "And these attacks are not helping in the least!"

G.E.M. knew they were doomed if they stayed like this. With no other choice, he turned towards Pinky. "Get us the hell out of here!"

"That's going to be tough Captain!" She yelled back at him. "They're trying to block us in!"

"Boomer!" He turned to his mute navigator, "Can you find us the weakest point in their hold?" Boomer wasted no time, rushing over to the radar screen for any sign of an opening.

As the bombardment continued, Victor called over the speaker. "The ship is starting to take heavy damage! If we stay here any longer, we are all going to fall right out of the sky!"

"Alan! Bob! Where is that cover fire?" He shouted at his gunners over the speaker.

"Hey!" Bob shouted back, "You try taking on six heavy duty Valen warships with only two cannons!"

"Yeah!" Alan added, "How about you get your butt up here some time?"

G.E.M. was starting to lose his temper from all the action going on "Boomer! Where is that opening?"

Boomer pointed at the top of the screen, showing a small opening between two ships that were right behind them.

"Is that really our only option?" G.E.M. questioned him, getting a nod in reply. "Fine." He said, hating the idea. "Pinky! I'm going to need you to turn us around and fly us out of here as fast as we can! Alan!" He shouted over the speakers, as the ship continued to be attacked. "I want you to focus your fire in front of us! We're going to need you to open the path as much as possible! Bob! Cover our backside so we do not get shot down while escaping! Victor! I need you to keep those engines running! Everyone else! Strap yourselves in! This is going to be a bumpy ride!"

"Yes! Captain G.E.M!" They all shouted.

"Get us out of here!" He commanded, and they were off.

Chapter 6

The Green-Eyed Monster seemed to charge towards the head ship in front of them.

"Have they gone insane?" The captain panicked, watching the Green-Eyed Monster coming right for him on the screen. "Are they planning on killing us along with themselves?"

"Turn us around now Pinky!" G.E.M. shouted his commands.

Pinky's gripped the controls tight enough to make her knuckles white. Screaming at the top of her lungs, she forced the controls to turn left, causing the entire ship to turn, and nearly throwing everyone on the bridge out of their seats.

The Green-Eyed Monster barely ran into the Valen war ship. The lower end of the Green Coat's ship scraped against the front ballast of the other.

G.E.M. and his crew clinked their teeth from the short, but painfully long scrapping that filled their ears.

Once they were turned around, Pinky stomped on the gas and punched a few buttons to blast them towards their exit point.

"What the…" The Captain stared, taking a moment to collect himself, before realizing what their plan was. Grabbing the closest mic, he shouted out to the other ships. "They are trying to escape! All ships! Blast them out of the sky! You two on the other side! Tighten up that hole! Don't let them escape!"

The Green-Eye Monster raced towards their only way out, watching it slowly closing up in front of them.

"Open fire on them Alan!" G.E.M. shouted his command through the speakers.

Alan slammed his thumb down the triggers, firing away at the two ships in their path. The cannon blasted away at the Valen ships, trying to keep them from closing.

"We're not going to make it like this!" Pinky shouted over the rushing roar of the ship.

"Then we're going to have to risk squeezing through!" G.E.M. ordered.

"What about the Princess?" Pinky asked her Captain. "We could all get crushed!"

"She's dead if we don't get out of here anyway!" G.E.M. argued, "Now quit arguing and get us the Void out of here!"

"Yes Captain!" Pinky agreed, preparing for the tight squeeze.

In the engine room, Victor was sweating bullets from the blazing heat they were giving off.

Now wearing a wielder's mask, heat resistant gloves, blue jean overalls, and a red and black flannel shirt, he tightens the bolts on the engine with his ratchet.

Another blast from outside forced him to catch himself on the engine. Looking over at the pressure index, he saw it was slowly going into the red. "Captain!" He called out over the speaker. "Whatever you guys got planned, you better do it now! I don't know if the engines can handle it much longer!"

G.E.M., Pinky, Sunshine, and Boomer watched as their exit kept getting smaller the closer they got.

"Now Pinky!" G.E.M. shouted, as Pinky turned the controls.

The Green-Eyed Monster turned on its left side, as it entered the closing space. About half way through, the hulls of the Valen ships pressed in on them, causing a terrible grinding sound to fill the halls of the Green-Eyed Monster, and the ears of the crew.

Sparks and metal scrapings went flying from the three ships grinding against each other. And by some miracle, they were able to get through.

It took thirty seconds to clear the path but felt more like thirty years of torture to the entire Green Coats crew.

Once they were though and straighten out, G.E.M. shouted, "Engines to overdrive right now! I want us out of the Valen's sights before they have any chance to chase us!

"Yes Captain!" Pinky shouted back, pulling down on a lever with all her might. The ships rockets made a massive boom, throwing G.E.M. and the others in the bridge back into their seat.

The clouds flew right by them; as they left the Valen fleet in their dust. They were there, and now they were not. They had to fly through some clouds, causing a bit of fear to pop in their heads that they might end up crashing into some other ship.

After a minute or two in overdrive, G.E.M. ordered Pinky to shut it off. She lifted the lever she had pulled, and the Green-Eyed Monster started to slow down.

Everyone was trying to catch their breath after what happened. Pinky's grip slowly slid off the controls, and she fell back into her chair, slowly closing her eyes. Sunshine was kind of the opposite, leaning over and gripping his keyboard. His knuckles were snow white from the tight grip, and his eyes bulging out.

Boomer was leaning in his chair as well. His breathing could be heard by the rest of the crew. He was human after all.

G.E.M.'s right hand gripped the chair's arm, while his left held his chest, feeling his heart beating faster than the ship had flown.

"Are we out of Valen's radar?" He asked in between breathes, looking over his crew.

Boomer was the first to respond to G.E.M. Looking at the radar system for any ships that may have followed them. He turned towards his captain, giving a *so-so* jester.

"Well…" G.E.M. responded sarcastically, "That is good for now."

Sunshine collected himself, typing away on his keyboard. "I'll send out a jamming signal to give us more cover, but those Valen ships are sure to be on our tail. We better keep moving if we want to make it out safely."

G.E.M. nodded approvingly at Sunshine before calling up Victor. "Please tell me the engines are still working."

"They are Captain," Victor told them, while looking them over. "But they are severely damaged from the overdrive and fire fight. We are going to have hide out in Zone-X for a good while, so I can fix them. Not to mention the rest of the ship"

"Get us moving Pinky." G.E.M. ordered.

"Just a heads up…" Victor called him, "I don't think we should use the overdrive again. Doing so or getting in another fire fight will kill the engines; then we will be joining it."

"You heard him Pinky." G.E.M. told her, "Take her nice and slow, but get us to Zone X as fast as you can."

"Wait Captain!" Victor cried out, but was interrupted

"Yes Captain!" She replied, grabbing the controls again, calming down a bit.

The ship slowly made its way through the skies, but still was able to go at a good speed. April, Alan, and Bob had joined them in on the bridge.

G.E.M. told them they were going to Zone-X, so Victor could fix up the ship, and they could sell off their bounty.

After a while, Pinky finally spoke up. "Are you going to check on the Princess?"

G.E.M.'s eyes widen at the realization. "Oh crap!" He undid his buckle, shot out of his seat, and rushed out to the storage room.

Opening the door, he saw that all the food and booze they had stolen was scattered all over the floor. It stained the walls and rugs.

"Damn it!" He cursed to himself. "Why did I not have them seal the crates?" He went in, looking over the mess.

All the fabrics and rugs were covered in stains.

G.E.M. sighed, rubbing the back of his head. "All that work for nothing." He kept looking around. "No one in Zone-X is going to want to buy this, or at least not at full price. Not to mention." He sighed once again, "At least we still have the jewelry I stole from the passengers on the upper decks."

Walking away, G.E.M. came to the bathroom he had the princess locked in. She was banging on the door, demanding to know what was going on, and G.E.M. opened the door.

Princess Zephyrus faceplanted onto the floor, in a mess. Her dress had water stains on it, possibly from the toilet. Her hair was messed up further, barely holding together now. And there were some bruises and cuts on her, possibly from getting bounced around from the firefight.

Seeing G.E.M. standing over her, she shot to her feet in righteous fury. "What the Void's going on?"

G.E.M. sighed, letting his breath collect, "You might want to follow me." He said and walked past her to the cargo hold.

It seemed most of the cargo was still intact. Some of the lighter boxes and chest had fallen over, but only the food container had spilled out. 'Maybe

May can do something with that.' G.E.M. thought to himself.

He walked over to a chest that had fallen over and set it back up. "You may want to sit down for this one Princess." He told her, getting back to his feet.

With a huff, Princess Zephyrus walked over, gracefully sitting down on her makeshift chair. "Now," She demanded in a proper tone. "Will you tell me what the Void happened?"

G.E.M. turned his head away from her for a moment, before turning it back to drop the bomb. "I got some sad news for you Princess." He told her, "It seems your adviser found out about your escape and has set up my crew and I for the fall."

"What are you talking about?" She asked him worryingly.

"We were caught in a Valen blockade," he explained, crossing his arms over his chest. "They showed us footage of the Leonardo having been completely destroyed, and everyone on board was murdered."

Princess Zephyrus gasped; hands over her mouth, her eyes widen in shock. G.E.M. had to ensure her that it was not his crew that did it, before she got the wrong idea.

"My crew has never destroyed an entire ship. Well... maybe some smaller ships." He told her, "But we have never blasted a cruise ship, or any large ships out of the skies. We'd fire on them to weaken their defenses, but never completely and utterly destroyed the ship. That would just destroy the cargo we want to steal. Nor would we waste or have the fire power on destroying it afterwards."

"Did you tell them I was on board?" She asked, looking up at him, pleading.

"That's the thing Princess." He looked her right in the eye. "They all think you died in the Leonardo's destruction."

Chapter 7

"That's not true!" She shouted at him.

"It is true Princess." He argued, "And what matters is what the Valen Kingdom thinks is true. Right now, they believe you were killed in our raid of the Leonardo." He looked away from her. "I do not know if they said you died from cannon fire, or if we shot you in the head. But they believe you are dead, and they are ordered to murder us all on sight."

"Why did you not tell them I was on your ship?" She kept shouting, getting to her feet.

"You think I did not try that!" He shouted back at her. "They did not want to listen to some 'lie' from a pirate! They wanted to blow up my entire crew and me!"

Princess Zephyrus stepped back, staring at G.E.M., before sitting back down, and crying into her hands.

G.E.M. looked away, not sure what else to tell the princess. Getting up to his feet, he made his way out of the room, stopping right at the hallway.

"My crew and I are heading to Zone-X to try to sell the goods we stole, and get our ship repaired. We also have some allies there that can get you to Hŭ Băi Hé."

Princess Zephyrus looked up at G.E.M. in shock of going to Zone-X. "Are you mad?" She shouted, running over and grabbing his jacket. "You can't go to Zone-X! The entire area is surrounded by a massive storm that never ends! Any ship that has tried to fly through it has never been seen again!"

G.E.M. questionably looked down at the princess, before showing a big toothy grin. "We pirates know of a secret path to the eye of the storm." He told her. "I assure you. We are not going to die. I still have a lot of sins to commit before I fall into the Void."

"So…" Princess Zephyrus asked, "You are going to help me?"

"Seeing how Valen has already charged us with your 'murder', killing you now would certainly be a death wish. By getting you to Hŭ Băi Hé, the bureaucrats there can show the Valen Kingdom that you're alive and drop the charges on us."

"So…" She asked, "what should I do in the mean time?"

He tugged his jacket out of her grip, taking a few more steps. "You can sleep with Pinky in her room. It is not like the silk linen sheets you are used too, but it is better than sleeping in that cramped chest."

"Okay." Princess Zephyrus said. "Can you show me?"

G.E.M. thought it over but sighed. "Okay." He agreed, "Follow me." He started walking down the hall, and she followed him.

As Princess Zephyrus was trailing behind the Captain G.E.M. he pointed out areas of the ship to her as she kept quiet.

"Starting on your left is the medical area." He pointed to a closed door. "Our doctor is April. I'd be careful around her." He explained.

"Why?" Zephyrus asked. "Is she dangerous?"

G.E.M. nervously shook a little, like a cold burst of wind hit him in the bare chest. "Let's just say… she likes cutting things."

Princess Zephyrus shivered as well, imagining a tall, demonic woman hiding in the shadows, with glowing blood red eyes and a sadistic, fang filled grin, while holding a scalpel and a saw.

Her thoughts were thankfully interrupted by the sound of a hatch opening. She leaned over to see around him, the floor lifted and one of the twins popped their head out.

"Can I get out of here now?" He asked his captain.

"Sure." Captain G.E.M. told him.

"Oh, thanks goodness." He said, rushing out of the hatch. "I got to pee." He rushed past them, going into the restroom without a second thought.

Princess Zephyrus was slightly embarrassed, but G.E.M. was fine. "Come on." He told her, before heading on.

Princess Zephyrus continued following G.E.M., but the sound of the guy in the bathroom sighing and doing his business behind a door was uncomfortable.

"Get used to it Princess." He told her, not looking at her. "You're going to have to take turns with everyone else on the ship."

Princess Zephyrus was shocked that she would have to share a restroom. "Isn't there another place?"

"There is my personal area." G.E.M. told her, "But that is MY personal area. But thankfully we have the showers located upstairs. You will have to shower with the other women on the ship however. We need to preserve our water."

Princess Zephyrus did not like the idea of having to share such a time with others, even if they were women. And after learning about the ships doctor, she was terrified.

"Don't worry about the guys." G.E.M. told her, not fully understanding why she was scared. "Boomer, Sunshine, and Victor are very respectable men, and Bob and Alan know better than to try anything that will get them killed."

"O-okay…" She responded, as they continued down the hall.

Something sweet soon struck their noses, as they approached an open door with some light coming out. A soft humming could be heard from it, somewhere between a melody and a lullaby.

G.E.M. stopped at the door, turning to face the princess, and leaned against the right side of the door to peek inside. Zephyrus looked in from the left, and saw May the cook, doing her role on the ship.

May was currently stewing something in a big pot on top of a stove. The kitchen area was not that wide. Just big enough for two people to get through without bumping into each other that much. The cabinets and drawers had locks on them to keep everything inside from falling out and breaking. The fridge was located at the end and seemed to be fastened to the floor.

The dining area took up the rest of the space. It was nothing more than a metal table and benches welded to the floor. It was large enough to seat a dozen people.

To G.E.M.'s surprise and joy, she did not seem all that bothered that they had almost gotten killed a little while ago.

May took a spoon full of what she was cooking and tasted it. Releasing a heavenly sigh, she reached into one of the cabinets, and added some pepper to it. "This will spice it up." She said, putting the pepper flakes back up and locking the cabinet.

"I see you're busy." G.E.M. finally spoke up, getting her attention.

"Oh Captain," she said, slightly startled. "It's nice to see you. And you as well Princess." She said, noticing Princess Zephyrus next to him. "I'm making dinner right now, and I will call you all down when it's ready."

"Thanks May." G.E.M. told her, starting to head out.

Princess Zephyrus started to follow him, but stopped when May called out to her.

"Princess Zephyrus, I know my cooking is nothing like the stuff you had back home, but I hope you enjoy it."

This made Zephyrus smile, as they continued.

The two went up a small set of stairs, before stopping at a metal door and another set of stairs that continued up.

"That is the bridge." G.E.M. explained, pointing at it with his thumb. "Please try avoid going in there."

"Why?" Zephyrus demanded.

"Because I don't need children running around in there." He bluntly told her.

Zephyrus just huffed, and they went upstairs.

"That's Alan and Bob's," G.E.M. pointed over the door closest to them on their left, as they stood at the top of the stairs. "Victor and Sunshine's, and Boomer has his own at the end." He explained, before pointing at the door on the opposite end of the floor. "That's my quarters. No one is allowed in there without my permission." He soon pointed to the rooms on the right. "That's Pinky's quarters, those are the showers I told you about, and that's April and May's."

"Wait!" Zephyrus stopped him, "How can you let that May girl stay in the same room as that cut happy doctor you told me about?"

"Easy," G.E.M. casually told her, "They're sisters."

Zephyrus could not believe what he was saying. How could such a sweet, kind person be related to monster she had imaged their doctor to be.

"Go on ahead and see about getting some sleep." He told her, starting to head down the stairs. "May will call everyone when dinner is ready."

"Why are you being so nice to me now?" She asked, stopping him in his tracks.

"I'm not." He told her, before looking right at her. "I'm just trying to make sure you keep your promise, once we hand you over to the Zǐ Sè Dēng Pào." And with that, he headed back down the steps, leaving the princess by herself.

Chapter 8

G.E.M. decided to check on the bridge, nearly crashing into Sunshine when opening the door. "What's up Sunshine?" He asked him.

"Oh good, you're here." Sunshine said, "Yves just released a press conference a minute ago." Sunshine rushed back to his keyboard to pull it up.

G.E.M. went to his chair, as the video started playing, showing Yves standing before the crowd. "I've just received word that the ship Princess Zephyrus was on was attack by the Green Coat pirates." He paused, lowering his head slightly. "They attacked the ship by jamming it signals and boarding it. Everything on the ship was stolen, before leaving, and blowing it up. There were no survivors reported, including Princess Zephyrus."

"How did they destroy the ship?" One person asked which Yves ignored till the next question came right after it. "Are they responsible for the King's death?"

"It is highly doubted that they are." Yves told them, "They are hardly ever seen on land, so they are not seen as the King's killer."

G.E.M. gave a soft sigh, "At least he is not blaming us for that."

"However," Yves seemed to reply to G.E.M.'s words. "They could be working with one of the enemy Kingdoms. Pirates like them have been known to be in league with Kingdoms that are used to attacking other Kingdoms' ships with little tying back to them. As such, we will be investigating this to see if the two events are connected."

The crowd called out to Yves as one voice shouted louder than the others, "What are you going to do about Captain G.E.M. and his Green Coats?"

Yves was silent for a moment, before slowly looking down at the man that asked, "We have the entire Valen armada hunting them down. There was even a report just before I came here telling me that Admiral Condor's fleet earlier had nearly captured them."

"Captured!" G.E.M. shouted at the screen, leaning forward in his seat. "That jackass nearly blasted us out of the sky!"

Yves continued talking to the crowd, "As suggested, we have raised the bounty on Captain G.E.M. and his crew to $100 million gold!"

Everyone on the Green-Eyed Monster gasped in shock at the mentioning of the new bounty.

"We even sent word to all our allies in Hŭ Băi Hé and Romeek about their crimes, and I have received their word that they will attack on sight." He added, before turning away. "Now if you'll excuse me, I must meet with the courts to discuss our plans for the King and Princess's funeral, as well as our kingdoms future." He walked away, with the video ending.

"That guy is full of bullshit!" G.E.M. shouted at the screen. "When was the last time we ever worked for any of those damn Kingdoms?" He looked over at Sunshine and Pinky in their seats, who looked over at him. "That's right! Never! We have never worked for any Kingdoms after they betrayed us. And I plan on keeping it that way, even if it kills me."

"Not to mention this is going to make it impossible for us to get the Princess to Hǔ Bǎi Hé." Pinky pointed out to them.

"Why is that?" Sunshine asked, turning to face her. "I thought Hǔ Bǎi Hé was a nation that is nonviolent."

"It is." G.E.M. explained, "But even they know that being 'nonviolence' could leave them subject to an attack by their neighbors."

"That is why they enlist the help of the Zǐ Sè Dēng Pào to help protect their trade ships and shores."

"Just like that ass Yves said," G.E.M. leaned back in his chair, still pissed. "Some pirates work with Kingdoms for various jobs. The Zǐ Sè Dēng Pào are just the prime example."

"So, they will attack us if we enter Hǔ Bǎi Hé air space." Sunshine realized, "Guess we cannot go to Zone-X then."

"Do not worry." G.E.M. ensured him, "We will be safe from them attacking us while in Zone-X. But I can't see it getting any worse."

The bridge door opened, as Victor walked in, wiping his hands. His clothing and skin had some oil and grime spots on it. "Seems I came at a bad time." He said, "But I hate to say it Captain, but the news does get worse."

G.E.M. groaned, laying his head into his palm. "What is it Victor?"

Victor took G.E.M. into the engine room, located behind the storage room. Pinky and Boomer stood behind G.E.M. as Victor explained the problem.

"That fire fight we got into with the armada has caused some considerable damage to the engines and the stabilizers." He pointed out to them.

They looked over at the engines. They were as tall as a person, about five feet. Heat radiated from them, causing sweat to start forming in their pores. In between them was a glass sphere with a few cracks forming around it that held a series of rotating rings inside.

"Can you fix them?" G.E.M. asked Victor.

"I can," he started to say, "but I need parts, and there were none in the loot we raided."

"What about getting us to Zone-X?" Pinky asked next.

"I won't be able to stabilize them enough while we're in the air." Victor explained, "But... if were we to land... I would be able to get to maybe 77%."

"We're still being hunted by the Valen, so landing anywhere would be dangerous." G.E.M. thought out loud for everyone to hear. "But maybe we could find an island with some cover to hide out in till you got the engines patched up. Boomer!"

Boomer slightly turned his head towards his captain. "Return to the bridge and see if you can find an island with a cave large enough for the Green-Eyed Monster or is densely forested."

Boomer nodded and headed off.

"Now…" G.E.M. said, looking right at the engines. "Let's just hope he can find something before we start falling from the sky."

Chapter 9

Princess Zephyrus sat in Pinky's sleeping quarters, wondering what was going to happen. She looked down at the dress she still wore. Once whiter than the clouds in the sky, now stained and covered in dirt and dust.

As she sat there, feeling like it had been hours, Zephyrus thought about her life and how it had become too much for her to handle, and she dropped her head into her hands to cry. Her Kingdom, her people, her grandfather; all of them were taken away by a man she once saw as her guardian angel.

The door opened, with Pinky seeing the young princess weeping before her. "Are you okay Princess Zephyrus?" She asked, coming up to her.

Zephyrus looked up at Pinky, her face like a mask, with her ruined make-up and dirt. She did not say anything, only sniffling and failing to hold back the tears that continued running down her young face.

"May I sit?" Pinky asked the princess, which the princess neither confirmed nor denied. "I'll take that as a 'yes'." She said sitting next to the princess.

"What do you want?" Zephyrus asked Pinky, as she sat there.

"I'm here to inform you that we may be taking a bit longer to get you to the Zǐ Sè Dēng Pào." Pinky started explaining.

"What?" Princess Zephyrus shouted in shock, looking up at her. "Why are you taking so long?"

"Our ship has taken some damage, and we need to land for a while to repair it." Pinky continued explaining to her calmly. "If we were to fly through Zone-X's winds the way we are now, we would all die. If we even made it there at all." She looked down at the princess's worried face, returning it with a smile. "But don't worry. Victor is the best mechanic in all the skies."

Princess Zephyrus did not say anything else. Just turned her head to stare at the wall.

"I was also going to ask if you'd like something to eat." Pinky explained. "G.E.M. and the rest of the crew are about to start, and I was wondering if you'd like to join us, so you could eat. Also, May made her world-famous soup."

"No thank you." She kindly declined, shaking her head.

"Okay then," Pinky got up, "I'll bring you something later, in case you do get hungry." She walked out, softly closing the door behind her.

With Pinky gone, Zephyrus fell over on the bed; her head hitting the pillow. Laying there in the silence of the room, her mind traveled back in time to better days.

Pinky went down to the first level and down the hall towards the dining area She could hear chatter and commotion becoming louder and louder, till she could see the rest of her crewmates in the light of the doorway.

When she walked in, she saw everyone talking. May was smiling, as she handed out plates of finely cooked food to Alan and Bob. The smell filled her nostrils with a sweet, warm aroma. Even with her eyes closed, she could see the roast beef surrounded by freshly cut fruit and drizzled in a tangy sweet sauce.

May had always made the best food, as far as Pinky was concerned. She always took great care with every dish she made. She cooked, with a passion, joy, and love that could not be matched.

She opened her eyes and noticed that Victor and Boomer were both missing from the table. 'Boomer must already be in his room.' She thought to herself, 'And Victor must still be working on the engine.'

"Hey Pinky," Victor walked in behind her, stepping aside to get past.

"Oh!" She realized she was in his way, and stepped aside to allow him through, "How are you doing?"

"I am doing alright." He smiled her. "I just wish I could say the same about the ship". He looked good, despite being covered in grime and oil. His hair was oily and messed up from working on the engines the entire time.

"Will we be able to make Zone-X in time for you to properly repair the ship?" Pinky asked, worried.

"I think we can, if we continue a slow and steady pace, and have the engine off for a day or two." He explained. "I just came down to get some food, before heading back to keep working."

"Alright." Pinky nodded and allowed Victor on his way.

After getting herself a slice of the roast beef, some fruits and vegetables, and some ale, Pinky sat down at the end of the table and started eating.

As she ate, she looked over at Alan and Bob catapulting their food at each other, trying to land it in the other's mouth. Alan pulled back on his fork with a carrot on it, while Bob hung his mouth open. The twin gunners lined up the shot and fired. The carrot flew through the air for a couple second before landing in Bob's mouth.

He ate it, while he and Alan threw their arms over their head to celebrate another perfect hit. They high-five each other, laughing at their greatness, before Bob set himself up to fire a piece of meat at Alan.

"I see our guest has decided not to join us." Pinky turned her head towards the head of the table to see G.E.M. staring at her.

"No." Pinky told him, looking back at her food. "I think she is still upset about everything."

"I understand." G.E.M. said, tossing an olive into his mouth. "She just lost everything that mattered to her. It's going to take some time before she can move on, if at all." He looked off in the distance.

"Are you sure about giving her to the Zǐ Sè Dēng Pào?" Pinky asked to get his attention.

"If I can talk to their captain, I am willing to think he will help us." G.E.M. explained, "But we are going to make sure the Princess is with us when we land. And I do not want to think what could happen if the other crews learn the Princess is still alive."

Pinky took a moment to think about it, before coming up with what G.E.M. was thinking. "Some of them would kidnap her, thinking they could get a big pay day from the people of Valen-"

"Only for Yves to have her killed in a 'rescue' attempt." G.E.M. finished her statement. "Not to mention those that would kill her for him, sell her into slavery, or gods know what else." He picked up a slab of meat and stuffed it into his mouth.

"And what makes you think the Zǐ Sè Dēng Pào will not do any of those things?" Pinky asked him.

G.E.M. chewed away on his food, making sure to swallow before speaking. "While they are pirates, like us; they are Lao Hu Bia He only line of defense from the other kingdoms." He explained. "Remember, the followers of Bu Er believe in non-violent. But the higher ups know that their neighbors do not follow the same principles. That is why they cut a deal with the Zǐ Sè Dēng Pào long ago to look the other way when it comes to their crimes on foreign ships, as long as they swear not to attack Hu Bia He ships and protect their lands when needed." He grabbed his cup, taking a long swig. Letting out a pleasant sigh, while wiping his mouth with his arm, G.E.M. continued. "Now days, the Zǐ Sè Dēng Pào are honor bound to protect Hu Bia He and help out when needed. I'm sure they will help us, if they do not try to kill us first."

Pinky just sat there, quietly thinking about all of it.

"Well," G.E.M. got up, "I think I will hit the showers, then turn in. It's going to be a long time till we reach Zone-X." He started to walk off, before stopping to look over his shoulder at Pinky. "Make sure Princess Zephyrus gets some food and drink in her. I do not want to hear her complaining the whole way." He then left Pinky there to enjoy the rest of the night.

As he was passing the bedrooms, he heard crying coming from the princess in Pinky's bedroom.

He went over, leaning his ear to the door. Crying could still be heard on the other side, as G.E.M. straightened himself up, and knocked.

The crying stopped for a moment, as he addressed her. "May I please come in Princess?" He asks, "I want to make sure you are alright."

"Go away!" She shouted at him from the other side.

"Are you sure you are alright?" He asked her once again.

"I'm just fine!" She continued shouting, "Now, go away!"

G.E.M. just stood there for a moment in silence. Shrugging his shoulders, he did as she told him, and entered his room.

The green jacket hung behind a towel on the rack, while the pants and shoes lay on the floor. Steam filled the whole room, while G.E.M. stood in the shower, hanging his head under it, watching as the blue water ran down the drain.

Giving off a tiring sigh, G.E.M. threw his head back and shook it to get some of the water out.

He turned off the showers and stood there a bit to let more of the water run-off, before grabbing a towel to dry off the rest and wrap around him. Getting out, he went over to the mirror, wiped off some of the fog that got on it, and stared into a pair of eyes that he had not seen in a while.

His throat wanted him to say something to his reflection, but his lips blocked the path. It was hard to address someone you never really like seeing without wanting to curse them to Void and back. "Whatever..." He sighed, finishing up before leaving his personal bathroom.

Back to normal, G.E.M. walked into his captain quarters. The first thing he saw when going inside was the full-size bed at the far end of the wall, in the middle. Next to the bed were two nightstands that had two lamps built into them, so they would not fall over. Looking over to his right, a full metal work desk stuck out of the wall. The chair under it was attached on the right side by a slide-and-lock system, just like how the draws worked as well. This allowed him to sit down, without having to worry about it falling over. On top of the desk was a lamp like the ones on the nightstand.

G.E.M. walked over towards the desk which showed a world map of the skies. It was covered by a glass surface, as a tiny model of the Green-Eyed Monster stood on the Valen's boards.

G.E.M. pulled out the seat to sit down and reached into his desk to grab some markers and a ruler.

Lining up one end of the ruler with the model, he lined the other end up with a large black circle located on the map labeled Zone-X. With one eye closed, he took a black marker, and drew along the edge of the rule, on top of the glass slowly.

When he was done, he looked down at the part of the map that show how long each centimeter on the map was a kilometer in real life.

G.E.M. looked back at the map, concluding, "Three days." He softly spoke to himself. "We just got to make it to Zone-X in three days, without running into any trouble. And pray Victor can keep us in the air as well."

He got up from his seat and when over to the left side of the room. On that side, there were two bookshelves filled with all different works of literature from all over the skies. Just like everything else, it was sealed to the wall to prevent it from falling over, and a glass door allowed G.E.M. to see his collection, while they were locked.

Between them was a dresser with a mirror sealed to the wall over it, and a hanger for his jacket. On the dresser was a green journal embroidered with the word "G.E.M." on it.

Picking up *his* journal, went over to his bed, and opened it to the first page that read "property of George Eliot Martin."

G.E.M. smiled and gave a single chuckle, before flipping it over to the last written page. "On this day, we were betrayed by our Kingdom. Me, my crew, and our ship are the only survivors of an ambush and set up that the Valen tricked our fleet to enter.

Now the Valen have declared that we betrayed them and the people. That we are the criminals and have put bounties on our head.

Well, if that's how they want to play it, then let us play the villains. We will be thorns in their sides, and no longer the shield that protect them from the real monsters.

We are the monsters now, and I am the one with green eyes.

And no one will feel safe when they see our ship but will instead be afraid when they see the Green Coats."

G.E.M. sighed, shutting the book. "And that continued on to this day Captain."

Chapter 10

G.E.M. woke up early, or he at least thought so. Throwing the covers off, he sat up, and stretched his arms out far and wide. Rolling towards the side of his bed, G.E.M. placed his bare feet on to the cold, metal floor. He was used to doing this, as he walks over to the dresser.

He changed into some fresh jeans, got his face ready for when the crew got up, and tossed his jacket over his shoulders like a cape.

Walking out the door, G.E.M. looked over to Pinky's door, knowing the princess was still in there with her. He was about to knock, but the princess's yelling last night and the fact they desired some rest made him rethink it.

G.E.M. continued down the hall, hearing the twins snoring when he passed by their door. Walking down the stairs, he decided to check on Victor and the engine.

The low hum could be heard as a dim orange glow could be seen when he got closer. G.E.M. stepped inside, checking it out. He could not understand how it worked, as metal covered the pipes, and wiring surrounding it.

Soft snoring came from the right corner of the room, causing G.E.M. to look over and see Victor sleeping. He was covered in oil and grime, 'probably from working on the engines all night.' G.E.M. thought to himself, smiling.

He kneeled next to Victor, grabbing his shoulder, and lightly shaking him. "Victor?" He whispered, "Wake up."

A mighty yawn came out of Victor's mouth, as he stretched out his arm over his head, and his eyes blinked a few times before fully opening. "Morning Captain," He yawned his greeting.

"How are the engines doing?" G.E.M. asked.

"Better." Victor replied, getting up. "It took me all night, but I'm sure we can make it to Zone-X. But I would still like for us to land, so I can double check, and make sure I didn't miss anything."

"How about you go get some sleep in your nice, soft bed for the rest of the morning?" G.E.M. suggested, "I'll have May bring you breakfast."

"No thanks Captain." He kindly declined, but a yawn escaped him. "I will get started on my morning routines, then take a shower to clean off."

"You can do that after you're fully rested." G.E.M. told him, "Now go to bed. That's an order."

"Okay Captain." Victor gave up, walking sluggishly down the ship's hall.

After that, G.E.M. went to the bridge to check on the autopilot. When he walked in, he was shocked to see Pinky sitting at the controls.

"Pinky!" G.E.M. called out in shock, "What are you doing up this early?"

"Princess Zephyrus took my bed." She answered.

"Really?" G.E.M. looked back up the stair, ready to give the princess an earful.

"Not really," She explained to him, before he could stomp off towards the princess. "I went to my room after everything was done and found her asleep in my bed. I decided to not disturb her so I came to the bridge to watch the autopilot."

"Did you get any sleep?" He asked, taking his seat.

"A bit." She said, "Maybe an hour or two." She yawned, showing she was still tired.

"Go get some sleep. That is an order." He told her. "I will take over for a while. Maybe you can get Sunshine or Boomer to take over."

Pinky yawned again, getting out of her seat. "Where will I sleep?" She chuckled

G.E.M. just smirked, "Take one of their beds." He told her, "But do not dare try to sleep in mine. I will know."

"Whatever you say, Captain." Pinky said, saluting him.

Before she left, G.E.M. remembered something. "Did Boomer ever find an island we could hide out on?"

Pinky stood at the door, looking over at him. "No such luck." She answered, "I even looked a bit, but couldn't find anything.

"Thanks Pinky." G.E.M. said, "Now go get some sleep."

Pinky did not say anything, but simply left the bridge.

All by himself, G.E.M. pressed a few buttons that were located at the end of his left armrest. The seat seemed to move around, as a joystick system moved out before him, and two petals rose out of the floor before his feet. Slowly gripping the joystick, G.E.M. gently pressed down on the gas petal.

He kept his grip on the joystick, keeping the ship straight. There were slight movements by his hand, but not enough to make the ship turn in anyway.

G.E.M. wanted his crew to get as much sleep as possible, especially after the near-death experience they had.

As he flew the ship, he watched the clouds softly fly by. Like little white piles of cotton that flowed in the sky.

Hearing a powerful yawn behind him, G.E.M. turned to see Sunshine walking in. "Morning Sunshine." He joked.

"Morning Captain." Sunshine stretched out his arms, while walking past G.E.M. to take his position.

"How was your night?" G.E.M. asked him.

"It was great." He told him, shaking whatever cobwebs were left in his head, before taking control of the ship.

With Sunshine taking over, G.E.M. allowed his controls to fold back in and sink into the floor. "I am going to make us some coffee." G.E.M. told him, getting up. "Would you like some?"

"I need some." Sunshine replied, looking over his shoulder at him.

"Okay." G.E.M. nodded back at him, looking over his shoulder as well.

The kitchen was mostly May's domain, but with her still sleeping, it was open to everyone.

Leaning against the counter, G.E.M. crossed his arms, as the coffee dripped into the jug. He had two cups set for him and Victor, as he waited. "I am sure we are out of Valen airspace by now." He told himself, "Or at least I hope." G.E.M. looked over at the coffee maker, knowing it was not going be long till it was done.

The coffee soon started pouring into the pitcher, dripping the whole time the sweet, warm aroma filled G.E.M.'s nose with caffeine and energy. Once it was done, he grabbed the two mugs and filled them up.

He took a sip of the coffee from his mug, letting the hot, bitter taste burn his tongue and wake him up, as he made his way back to the bridge.

G.E.M. walked in, seeing that Boomer had already joined Sunshine on the bridge, checking the radar for any danger. "If I knew you would be awake by now, I would have poured a third cup."

Boomer did not say anything, just writing something down for G.E.M. and Sunshine about the weather.

G.E.M. took it, reading it to Sunshine. "Looks like we are in the clear." He told him, "No sign of any ships in any direction. If we keep this up, we will make it safely to Zone-X in two more days. But there are still no signs of any islands close by for us to make a pitstop."

"That is good." Sunshine said. "We don't need another attack today."

"But Victor would still like to work on the engine when it is not running." He pointed out to Sunshine. "Keep making sure no one comes our way but look out for any islands we can rest on." G.E.M. told Boomer, "We are still being hunted by the Valen Kingdom, and their allies are bound to be on the lookout for us."

After a while, the rest of the crew got up. May made everyone a small breakfast, Victor did his daily routine of checking over the ship, April went to the medical room, Alan and Bob came down to get their food then headed back to their room, and Pinky came back to the bridge after she got her rest.

The only one that was not there was Princess Zephyrus. "She's still locking herself in your room?" G.E.M. asked Pinky. Who was sitting in her seat next to Sunshine at the controls.

"Yeah," Pinky nodded.

G.E.M. rubbed the top and back of his head in frustration. "Well… At least it will keep her out of trouble."

"You are right." Pinky agreed, "But are we really going to keep her locked in there forever?"

"Is she eating?" G.E.M. asked.

"She did." Pinky said.

"Then we do not have a problem." G.E.M. told her.

"YOU do not have a problem." Pinky corrected him, "I get to see her every time I enter my room. Not to mention I am the one that has to comfort her when she starts wondering if she will live."

G.E.M. sighed, hating when Pinky was right.

"And I would like to get my own bed, back sometime soon." Pinky continued.

"Alright." G.E.M. gave in.

G.E.M. got up, turning to see the princess peeking from the other side of the door. "How long have you been there?"

"Not… Not long." Princess Zephyrus nervously replied.

"Well," G.E.M. did not see any other option, seeing how they were all stuck on this ship together, till they reached Zone-X. "You want to join us here on the bridge?"

Zephyrus quietly entered, not knowing what was going to happen. Her eyes looked around, seeing the complex yet simple set up that controlled the Green-Eyed Monster. She looked around, taking in the entire place.

"You like?" He asked.

Zephyrus did not say anything, but slowly walked around to check things out. She came over to Boomer, looking over at the radar screen.

"That's the radar." G.E.M. told her from his captain's chair. "And over there by Pinky and Sunshine, those are the controls and systems of the ship."

"It takes two people to control the ship?" Zephyrus asked.

"No." G.E.M. replied, "There are just two different controls, so one can take over without the other having to give up their seat. Also… Sunshine sits there so he can hack into anything we need."

"Like Valen ships?" Zephyrus said.

"Well… Yes…" He spoke.

Zephyrus stared directly at G.E.M. with ill will.

"Hey!" G.E.M. shouted, knowing exactly what Zephyrus was thinking. "If it wasn't for us, you would be dead! Or worse!"

"What could be worse than death!" Zephyrus shouted.

"A lot of things are worse than death! Just ask the original G.E.M.!" He yelled at the top of his lungs.

"Okay…" Sunshine jumped in, wanting to end the racket. "How about we have the Princess go to the kitchen and see if May has something sweet for her?"

G.E.M. did not reply to Sunshine's suggestion right away. "Fine." He finally answered, "Get out of here, before I get really mad."

Princess Zephyrus just huffed and walked right out the door.

With her gone, G.E.M. told Boomer. "Find us an island as soon as you can. Once Victor repairs the engine enough to give us a survivable chance against Zone-X's powerful winds, we might just leave that brat on that island."

With that, G.E.M. leaned back into his chair, fuming.

Chapter 11

"That barbaric jerk!" Princess Zephyrus shouted, storming down the first level. The small tight space felt claustrophobic compared to her old home in the palace. It was also darker and grayer than the bright, white marble pillars and walls, the tile floors covered with gorgeous patters full of blues, greens, whites, and other colors of the rainbow.

Her steps slowly come to a stop, at the thought of missing home. She couldn't deny she hated it here, being stuck with these pirates.

Her thoughts were broken when she felt a strong whiff of something cooking tickled her nose. She turned her head towards where the sweet, tangy aroma was coming from, finding May working in the ship's kitchen.

May was happily humming along, as she swung the pan over the store back and forth. The food inside tossed and turned like a wave, but she never lets a single crumb fall out of the pan.

The Princess walked into the dining area, slowly making her way over to May. As she got next to the cook, she stood there quietly, kindly waiting for May to either stop what she was doing, or after she was finished. Luckily for her, it was the former, as May caught the princess out of the corner of her eye.

"Oh," She greeted, "good morning Princess. Did you sleep well?"

Princess Zephyrus did not respond.

"Okay…" May said, "Are you hungry? Would you like some breakfast? I may not be like the cooks back home, but it's really good."

Princess Zephyrus thought about it for just a second, before she nodded. "Yes, I would like some." She said, "What are you cooking?"

"Just some leftovers from last night." She explained. "It helps save on food, and you won't believe how tasty some things are a second time."

Princess Zephyrus could not believe her nose, what a wonderful smell coming from May's pan. How could last night's food smell so good. 'I bet it doesn't taste as good.' Zephyrus thought. But soon, her stomach growled like an angry dog ready to bite her if she tried to fight it.

"How about you take a seat at the dining table?" May suggested. "I think most of the crew skipped out, or already got something, but April is in there! How about you go sit next to her? I don't think you two have formally met yet. Alan and Bob are in there as well, waiting for their breakfast."

Princess Zephyrus's eyes shot open at the idea of meeting April, May's sister for the first time. After what she heard about April, Zephyrus did not want to meet her.

"Oh…" May said, staring at Zephyrus with a cute expression on her face, mistaking Zephyrus' fright. "You must be shy. How about I introduce you to her?"

Before Princess Zephyrus had the chance to tell her 'No', May was pushing her from behind, leaving the still cooking pan on the stove.

Zephyrus saw the metal table, with the three sitting there quietly. April was humming to herself, while she scraped her knife along her fork.

Alan and Bob were strangely quiet, as if making a peep would waken some kind of monster.

"Hey sis!" May called out to April, getting her attention. Zephyrus could see the family resemblance with the two close to each other. "This is Princess Zephyrus of the Valen Kingdom! She's the girl I told you about last night."

April looked over at Zephyrus, giving a kind, yet uneasy smile. "It's nice to finally meet you properly, and G.E.M. 'kidnapped' you. Come," She said, patting the empty spot next to her. "Have a seat."

Zephyrus did not want to but felt not doing so would be dangerous to her health. So, she sat down next to April, while May went back to the kitchen.

Zephyrus nervously sat there, wondering what to do and say to the three others sitting around her. Her eyes glazed over at Alan and Bob, who looked over at her with equal amounts of worry.

"My sister told me that you're trying to get to Hǔ Bǎi Hé." April spoke up, causing Zephyrus to jump a bit in her seat.

Zephyrus was not sure how to respond, only giving a long "A…" She hung on that for thirty seconds, before she started speaking. "Yes. I need to get to Hǔ Bǎi Hé for protection."

"Isn't G.E.M. such a wonder man?" She stated, giving a dreamy sigh. "I would love to know what makes him tick."

"'Wonder man'?" Zephyrus questioned April's idea of him. "'Makes him tick'?"

Alan and Bob's eyes both widen in terror. Alan waved both hands in front of his face, while Bob swung his right hand along his neck like a blade.

"You completely agree with me." April said, not realizing Zephyrus was questioning her statement about G.E.M. and not praising him.

"Yes… If it wasn't for him, who knows where May and I would be."

"What?" Zephyrus asked, as May walked in.

"Here's breakfast!" She called out, carrying four bowls on a metal tray in her palm. Walking around the table, she placed a bowl in front of everyone.

Zephyrus forgot about her conversation with April, as she looked at the food before her. The visible, ghostly steam raising out of the bowl made it perfectly clear that it was piping hot. She leaned over it, inhaling the warm vapor from the bowl.

Her insides filled with the warm, savory air, and her stomach cried out for the warmth of the food in the bowl. But her eyes told her not to eat it. It was a hash posh of chopped meat of different animals. There was chicken, beef, and a bit of pork, along with random fruits and vegetables.

"Growl growl!" Zephyrus heard, looking up from her bowl to see Alan and Bob wolfing down their food like mindless savages. The sight of them holding the bowls over their faces, as the soup spilled on their cloths disgusted her to no end.

"Hey!" April shouted, stopping the two from eating, as she threw a scalpel into each of their bowls, frightening the twins and Zephyrus. "We have a guest. I expect both of you to eat like civilized pirates."

Both gunners slowly lowered their bowls, showing the pure terror on their faces, before gulping what they had left in their mouths. "S-sorry April." Bob apologized. "S-sorry Miss Princess Zephyrus." Alan did the same thing.

"Now," April said, turning to face the princess. "We were taking about how wonderful of a gentleman G.E.M. is."

Zephyrus looked up at April with fright but found the courage to speak her mind loud and clear. "You people are insane!"

Everyone paused, except May, who was picking up the bowls her sister just ruined. "I'll take those off you boys. Let me know if you want seconds."

April finally spoke, talking the princess by surprise. "Maybe we are. But in this world, you need a little insanity to survive."

"There is no way that man is as great as you say he is." Princess Zephyrus told April right to her face.

April shot right out of her seat, staring down at Zephyrus with murderous intend. "How dare you speak ill of our Captain!"

Zephyrus realized too late her mistake, as April pulled out another scalpel, and nearly cut her with it. Alan and Bob rushed over to the other side, holding April back before the blade could cut Zephyrus.

"Don't kill the Princess!" Alan warned her.

"Why shouldn't I?" April shouted, fighting against the twins. "We're already charged with her death!"

"But we need her alive to hand over to the Zǐ Sè Dēng Pào!" Bob told her.

Zephyrus felt someone grabbing her shoulder from behind, looking back to see May smiling over her. "Let's get out of here." She said, dragging her out of the room and away from her crazy sister.

Zephyrus was dragged out to the kitchen, through the hall, and taken to the storage area of the ship.

Once they were there, May leaned down, staring Zephyrus eye to eye. "Never. I repeat. Never! Insult the Captain in front of her. She loves him."

"Why would she love someone like him?" Zephyrus demanded to know.

"Well..." started, "If it wasn't for him... my sister and I wouldn't be here."

"That's obvious." Zephyrus told her, crossing her arms.

"I mean," May told her, "He saved our lives." May walked over to one of the boxes, sitting down and patting the spot next to her. "I'll explain everything."

Princess Zephyrus sat next to her, as May began talking.

Chapter 12

April and I grew up on the island in the middle of Zone-X. We didn't know who our father was. We may have even had two different fathers, but that didn't matter to us.

Our mother... she worked at the brothels as a... well you can guess what she did there.

She worked hard to make sure we had enough to eat, but we were forced to care for ourselves most of the time.

We lived in a rat-filled little shack on the poorest side of the island. Every day, the roaring winds of the storm that surrounded our island tried to tear down our home. Our clothes were filthy and had holes in them. Void, I'm not even sure one could even consider them as clothes.

I did what I could to make our rotten hole into a home and slowly discovered my love for cooking, thought I was terrible at it at first. I would cook anything I could find, believing it would help us. Any food, no matter how rotten it was. It was good enough for us.

April was the one that protected me from those who tried to harm or kidnap us. I always remember seeing something sharp in her hand. A knife, a sharp rock, some broken glass, it was always something like that in her hand, covered in blood. It frightened me so much at times, but she would always tell me. "Don't worry May. It's going to be alright."

She soon started bringing in money as well, but I'm certain that it wasn't made honestly. Not that our mother's work could be called honest as well.

I think she learned how to do medicine by treating herself all the time. We didn't have anything too fancy, but she would dip her injuries in hot water and use old rags to cover them.

Our mother would bring home some money, but she always looked so broken and hollow. It was like a piece of herself was missing or taken little by little every day.

There were days she would be sick, but still leave for work. April would even tell her that she didn't have to keep doing what she was doing anymore, but she would keep going to try to earn us money.

Soon however... she didn't return. First it was a night, then a few days, after a week we went out looking for her throughout the entire island.

We... found her, but she was dead. She had been dead for days by the way she smelled. I broke down, crying more tears than I knew my eyes could shed.

April, on the other hand, she cried out in bloody murder. Rage, anger, and hatred filled her. She demanded that I return home right away.

I told her that I didn't want to leave her. We had just lost our mother, and I didn't want to lose her as well. But she was demanding, and I coward away from her, making my way back.

I don't know what she did, and in truth, I never what to find out. All I know is that I was in our shack, still crying when she returned. I looked at her and saw she was covered in cuts and sores.

She said, "mother can rest peacefully now."

I almost asked her what she meant, but my fear choked the words in my throat.

After we got older, I started working as a barmaid. It was a good thing I knew how to cook, but there was always some guy trying to hit on me. I always told them that if they didn't behave themselves, I would tell on them to April.

Most wouldn't listen and would end up regretting it later. I would see them again, but they would make sure to leave me alone.

April's love for cutting grew, and she decided to be a butcher. But none of the butchers on the island wanted her as an apprentice because she was a woman, so she settled for being a surgeon's assistant.

One day, after my sister got off work, she visited me at the tavern where I was working. We didn't notice at the time, but that's when G.E.M. first showed up.

He sat down, and I waited on him.

"Give me the house special." He ordered, "And some rum."

"Yes sir." I told him, making sure to take it down.

As I was doing that however, one of the few men that April had… taught a lesson to, showed up and sat close by as well.

I don't know what they were talking about, but April explained it to me.

He was bald and had a large cut going across his face. He told her, "Remember me?" He wore button-up shirt and trousers.

She looked over at him and said, "I recognize the cut, but sadly I've done dozens of those."

"Maybe this will jog your memory." He said, ripping his shirt open, and showing off dozens of cuts and slashes crisscrossing all over his body.

"Oh yes!" She recognized him. "You're that bastard that groped my sister about a month ago. I see the cuts have healed up nicely. How's that hand? Were you able to get those fingers reattached, or did you have to get prosthesis?"

I came out from around the bar about that time with G.E.M. meal and drink. "Here you go sir." I said, setting it down before him.

"Thank you." He said, before asking, "Who's the couple?" He pointed over at April and the guy.

I looked over shocked. "April!" I called out, rushing over to her.

April looked over towards me, as did the guy.

"I remember you." He said, frightening me. "You're the reason I'm like this!"

I thought he was going to attack me, but April got between us. "This is between you and me."

"Now it's between you two and us." He said, snapping his fingers. All around the bar, men started to get up from their chairs and surround us. They all had cuts and slashes on their faces. If I remember correctly there were... fourteen.

I coward behind April, while she got a knife out to fight. One of the men grabbed me by the arm and pulled me away from April, before she noticed.

All I could do was look at her, while his forearm wrapped tightly around my neck. "Put the knife down, or your sister will die."

"Just kill her right away!" Another one of the them shouted, terrifying me.

The only thought I had was that I was going to die, before I heard a gun go off, and the man holding me let go. April and the men all looked my way in shock, while I was confused.

"I came here looking for dinner, not a show." I heard G.E.M. speak up, causing all of us to look his way. "And it takes fourteen men to fight two women?"

"Don't you know who this is?" One of them asked, "This is April the Butcher. She cuts up anyone she doesn't like, not to mention she stole from all of- "

G.E.M. just shot him in the head, before he could finish his sentence. "And I'm Captain G.E.M.

of the Green Coats, looking for a new cook for my crew. I welcome you to Zone-X, where the only way to survive is to be strong. Or ruthless."

Without a warning, the remaining men all pulled out their guns and started to open fire on G.E.M.

He quickly knocked over and hid behind his table, surviving gun fire.

I ran behind the bar top, hiding away. April was quick, attacking some of the men with her knife, cutting, and stabbing them.

I don't know all the details, but from what April told me, her and G.E.M. were amazing. When the remaining men turned their guns on April, she jumped behind the table with G.E.M.

As I was hiding behind the bar top, I grabbed for the closest thing I could reach for. I grabbed a full bottle of rum, holding it by the bottle neck. It's a good think I grabbed it, cause right then, one of the men grabbed me by my hair and started pulling it.

I closed my eyes, swung as hard as I could, and hit him right in the head, breaking the bottle.

He let go of my hair, and I peeked over the top to see that April and G.E.M. had taken care of most of them. April had just stabbed one of the last two standing in the heart, but the other was getting readying to shoot her in the back.

G.E.M. got his attention by shouting "Hey!" Causing him to look over at G.E.M.

G.E.M. finished him off, first by shooting him in the knees to get him lower to the ground, then shooting him in the arm, and finally, rushing over, using the tips of his cutlasses to hand stand on the man's head, he then shot him nearly point blank in the eyes.

April and I watched the whole thing in shock, surprise, and wonder. It was like watching a flowing dance of death.

With the whole thing over G.E.M. turned to us. "I originally came here looking for a cook but looks like I only found trouble."

My eyes popped wide open. "I'm a cook!" I shouted rushing over to him.

"Did you make the meal I just ate?" He asked right to my face.

"Um, well, no." I admitted.

"Good." He said, "That stuff tasted terrible. You're hired."

I shouted and cheered, jumping around with excitement, before realizing that I would be leaving April alone. "Can my sister come with us?" I asked him.

He looked over at her. "Well… we do need a new doctor as well."

"I know how to cut things open." April told him.

"Um… do you know how to bandage and treat wounds?" He nervously asked her.

"More or less." She said, "And if you try to take May without me… you'll see just how good of a doctor I can be."

With one final gulp, G.E.M. agreed to have us both become members of his crew, and we've stuck with him and the others ever since.

Chapter 13

G.E.M. was sitting in his chair, when he felt a tap on his shoulder. Turning to see who it was, Boomer's mask covered face looked back at him. "What do you want?"

Boomer signed *found an island.*

"That' good to hear." G.E.M. told him. "Have Sunshine put it up on screen."

Boomer nodded, leaving G.E.M. to go back to his area.

After a few moments, Sunshine pulled up the picture of the island Boomer found onto the screen. It was perfect for them to hide out on for a while and have Victor fix up the engines into better shape. It floated in the sky. The jagged ground and rocks of the bottom and the lush, green forest on top gave it a green ice cream appearance in a cone.

G.E.M. stood up, shouting his orders with pride. "Find us a good clearing to land, one that can cover us in case anything comes near!"

"Yes Captain!" Pinky and Sunshine shouted back.

G.E.M. called up Victor in the engine room. "We got some good news Victor. We just found ourselves a place to hide out for a while to give you the chance to fix up the engines."

"Thank goodness." Victor told him.

G.E.M. leaned back into his chair, smiling as he whispered to himself. "Now I wonder if she could survive here by herself, till we get Zǐ Sè Dēng Pào to pick her up."

The ship slowly hovered over the island, finding a clearing large enough for it to land. As it lowered itself down to the ground, four landing pads appeared from under the ship, allowing it to land without damaging the turret gun on its stomach.

Once the ship was grounded, Victor waited a bit for Sunshine to turn off the engines. It was easy to do. Just flip a few switches, turn a couple keys, and shut off the power. With that done, G.E.M. had the crew gather together to decide who would stay to defend the ship and who would be exploring the place for food, water, and possible threats.

G.E.M. stood before the crew, who were lined up in order of Pinky, Boomer, Alan, Bob, April, May, Princess Pain-in-neck, Sunshine, and Victor.

"Okay." G.E.M. stated, "I'm going to be leading a scouting party, while the rest stay here to defend the ship while Victor is working. Alan. You're with me. Bob. You stay."

The twin gunners groaned, hating G.E.M.'s decision. "Come on Captain." Alan complained.

"You spilt us up every single time we do this." Bob added to his brother's complaint.

"That's because I can't keep both of you on the ship without me, and I can't handle the two of you when we're outside. Now shut it!"

They both shut their mouths, not wanting to risk his wrath.

"Pinky. With me. April. You stay." G.E.M. continued.

May noticed how April was staring daggers at the princess, even after she told the princess their story, but had not informed April that she shared their story.

"Um…" May spoke up. "Maybe April should be part of the scouting party?"

G.E.M. glared at her with firmness and surprised wrapped up in one.

"Um…" May tried to speak up more. "April's knife skills will be better suited for the forest environment, than Pinky's guns."

Pinky looked over at the three other women, noticing in each of their faces why May wanted this. "I agree with her Captain. We need someone to stay in charge of the ship, in case there is an attack. We don't know how long you'll be out, and Bob and I would protect the ship better than him and April."

G.E.M. groaned, seeing the logic in his first mate's plan. "Fine… you can stay. April. You are with me."

April's eyes turned towards G.E.M., giving him a sly smile.

"And finally…" He said, looking at Boomer and Sunshine, trying to decide who would go where. Boomer would be good for the scouting party. He was a good fighter, and navigation was his specialty. But that would only leave two real fighters on the ship.

On the other hand, Sunshine was a hacker, not a fighter. If there was any danger on this island, he would be a liability. There was also the fact that he worked the ship better than anyone else if they needed to make a quick escape.

G.E.M. finally remembered the turret on the ship's belly. If anyone did attack the ship, he could just jump in there to help defend it.

"Boomer, you are coming with me." G.E.M. decided. "Sunshine stay on the ship, in case we have to leave early."

"Yes Captain." Sunshine agreed, with Boomer just nodding.

G.E.M. slightly smiled, happy there was no complaining or arguing with this one.

"What about me?" Princess Zephyrus spoke up.

G.E.M. looked at her. While he would love to take her with them in the hopes that she would get separated from the party and hopelessly lost, he knew Pinky and May would be against him leaving her.

"You are to stay here." He told her. "We don't know if we're the only ones on this island. If there is anyone else, we also don't know how they are going to react to seeing you."

That was the end of the argument, as G.E.M. turned his back and headed up to the hatch with Boomer, April, and Alan lined up behind him.

Reaching over to press on the side of the hatch, it started to open by swinging outwards and forming a ramp.

G.E.M. turned back to the crew watching the ship. "We'll make our way back by sunset at the latest. Everyone got their communicators?"

Everyone nodded, including Boomer who only used his by sending codes.

"Then let us head out." G.E.M. ordered, leading the scouting party.

The forest was thick, making the four push branches out of their way. The ground was covered with dead leaves and twigs crunching under their feet as they walked.

This was one of those few time G.E.M. wished he had worn a shirt, as his bare chest consistently rubbed against the fresh green leaves and their branches.

"Maybe we can find some water." G.E.M. suggested, "Or possibility some food. I wish I had noted our rations before we left."

Just then, Boomer's head jolted up, hearing something. He stopped in his tracks, getting the attention of the other members.

"Hm…" G.E.M. looked over at Boomer, having stopped in his tracks as well. "What it is?"

Boomer put his index finger over where his mouth should be, indicating that they should be quiet.

"What is-" Alan started to say, before Boomer covered Alan's mouth with his hand.

Boomer then looked to his right and signed them to follow, before taking out his bladed boomerang and carefully walking off to not make too much noise.

"What's his deal?" Alan complained, before meeting S2BU before his eyes.

"Shut up." G.E.M. ordered in the quietest, yet threating voice he could muster. "He heard something. So, get your guns out and be ready for a fight."

With that, G.E.M. followed behind Boomer with both guns drawn. April walked behind G.E.M. twirling her scalpel for fun, while Alan annoyingly shrugged and made up the rear with his gun out and ready.

As they followed Boomer, they started hearing a series of voices that sounded as if they were singing. The closer they got, the clearer the sounds became and started to form a song of some kind.

"Cut them open just like a fish/ Serve their heads upon a dish/ Rip their hearts out of their chests/ The most blood on them is best!" The voices sang, sending a chill down nearly everyone's spines.

They stopped in their tracks, looking at each other in fright as the song continued.

"Link by link we carry our sins/ Soaked blood red from all our wins/ Romeece men hear rattling chains/ Fear grips them with Badrick's name!"

Boomer looked at all of them, signing, *"We got to get out of here."*

No one disagreed, not wanting to get an inch closer but instead miles away.

They were about to move, when a loud scream came from their left. Looking over, the four were surprised by a thin man wearing pants made from animal hide and some chains wrapped around his arm jumping at them, holding a war ax over his head to attack them.

Chapter 14

All four of the Green Coats jumped out of the way of the attacker's ax being swung down towards their heads. Boomer and G.E.M. going to the attacker's left, and Alan and April going to his right.

April reached for one of her scalpels, but Alan beat her to the punch by pulling out his gun and shooting the attacker right in the chest.

"No don't!" G.E.M. shouted over the loud bang of Alan's gun going off.

The attacker stood there a moment, before slowly dropping dead to the ground.

The attacker laid there between them. He wore dirty, ragged loincloth made from animal hide. Shackles were clamped on his wrists, with long chains wrapping up his arms that were stained with dried blood.

They did not have time to let it sink in, as shouting and rustling caused G.E.M. to order "Everyone back to the ship!"

Everyone, but Alan, followed right away, running back the way they came without a second thought.

"What's going on?" Alan questioned them, before G.E.M. forced him to start running by pulling on the collar of his coat.

"You just killed a Red Chain!" G.E.M. shouted, "And just alerted the rest of his team to our presence! Now we could end up dead!"

At that very moment, a tomahawk flew right between them, striking a nearby tree.

G.E.M. wasted no time calling up Pinky. "Get the ship ready."

"What the Void is going on?" She asked. "Victor barely got started on the engine."

"We just ran into some Red Chain pirates, and they are right behind us!" G.E.M. panickily told her.

Pinky did not reply right away. G.E.M. hoped that meant she was rushing to the hatch that very moment.

As he was waiting, a piercing pain struck G.E.M. in the back, causing him to fall over. The rest of the crew stopped, turning to see an arrow sticking out of his lower back on the right side.

"Captain!" April rushed over. She threw his arm over her shoulders and help to lift him up.

While that was going on, Alan and Boomer noticed Red Chains that were coming after them. There were ten to twenty of them. Their chains rattled, clinked, and chimed as they got closer.

April dragged G.E.M. behind one of the trees, as Alan and Boomer ducked behind trees of their own. "We can't get to the ship fast enough with our Captain like this!" April shouted over to them.

"Then what are we going to do?" Alan shouted, taking a few shots at the charging force, before having to hide behind his tree once again to avoid a volley of arrows and two tomahawks.

Boomer seemed to be taking his sweet time, trying to aim his boomerang for the perfect angle.

April took out her scalpels to get ready to protect her Captain. "Isn't this wonderful?" She asked G.E.M.

"Yeah," G.E.M. sarcastically said. "We're going to die by another pirate crew, and one that's known for killing nearly everyone they attack. And here I am, about to die in your arms."

"I know. Isn't it great?" April proudly exclaimed, while checking out her blades.

G.E.M. groaned, but was not sure if it was from the pain or the fact that April was going to be the last person, he would see alive.

While that was going on, Alan continued firing his guns, till they were only clicking. He hid back behind his tree for cover and shouted, "I got most of them, but I'm out of bullets!"

"How many?" April asked him.

Alan risked getting attacked by looking at the coming Red Chains to get a number. "I see about three."

"We can handle this." April told G.E.M.

Boomer threw his boomerang at that moment. It swirled through the woods, not letting anything get in its way. It cut through twigs and branches, curving around.

The remaining Red Chains did not see the blade coming, as it flew around, and decapitated all but one of them that had a metal shackle around his neck. The boomerang struck hard, causing the Red Chain to stumble.

"Wait here." April told her Captain, as she got up and dropped his head to the ground.

"Ow." G.E.M. moaned, carefully reaching behind his head to rub the pain away.

April jumped out from behind the tree and charged at the Red Chain at full speed. With scalpels in hand, she jumped over him and threw all of them, killing him as one struck him in the heart right above where some of the chains crisscrossed.

With the Red Chains dead, G.E.M. was able to hobble over thanks to Boomer going over to him and holding him up.

"We need to get out of here." G.E.M. told them. "If Badrick finds out that we killed some of his men, we'll end up just like those two." He pointed over at the two decapitated bodies lying on the ground.

"Should we at least see what they were doing here?" Alan asked.

G.E.M. glared daggers at him. "I don't want to spend another second on an island the Red Chains are on! We got to get out of here pronto!"

G.E.M. turned towards the ship with Boomers help and hobbled back. Alan and April just looked at each other for a moment, before walking behind their captain.

Pinky and Bob were waiting for the four, as they came up the ramp to board the ship. They were shocked when they saw G.E.M. still had the arrow in his side. Rushing over, Pinky helped Boomer haul G.E.M. up. "We need to get you to the med bay right away."

"No…" G.E.M. groaned in protest. "I'm… fine…" He leaned over, barely staying up.

"No, you're not." Pinky told him, before ordering Boomer. "Help me get him to med bay right away. April, come with us." She ordered April.

"With pleasure." April said with a smile on her face.

Once G.E.M. was brought into the med bay, they got to work by having him take his coat off first. Using some wire cutters, they snipped off the arrowhead and quickly pulled the rest of it out from his back.

G.E.M. tried to grit his teeth so as not to scream, but the pain was too much for him to hold back.

April grabbed some alcohol from her cabinet and rushed it over. Putting the alcohol on two sperate rags, she and Pinky pressed them both into the wounds to cover them. This in turn caused G.E.M. to curse and scream.

"Get me the bandages!" April ordered Boomer.

He wasted no time getting them, and handed them to April, who in turn had him hold the rag she was holding. She then proceeded to walk around G.E.M., wrapping the bandage around his stomach area like she was trying to dress him up as a mummy.

"Why were the Red Chains here?" Pinky asked during the bandaging. "How did Sunshine or Boomer not pick them up on their reading?"

"We'd have to ask them that." G.E.M. said, glaring at Boomer, who flinched in one of the few times in his entire life. "As for why they were here... I don't know. Maybe they were burying some treasure,"

"Treasure?" Bob asked, popping his head in the doorway.

"I heard treasure." Alan jumped in.

G.E.M. just looked at them with the same glare. "Or many they were burying some bodies there."

Alan and Bob's faces drained to ghost white, just before vanishing from view just as quickly.

"There's a number of reasons why they could be here, and I don't want to stay long enough to find out." G.E.M. continued, "And speaking of 'finding' out, if Badrick finds out we killed his men, we're all dead, and WHY THE HELL ARE WE NOT TAKING OFF!"

"Victor needed to fix the engines." Pinky told him.

"We don't have time for him to fix them." G.E.M. said.

"And done." April interrupted, finishing the wrapping. "It's too bad it wasn't a bullet. I would be able to see what makes you tick." She slapped his back.

"Ah!" G.E.M. screamed, bending his spine nearly in half. "Let me see Victor and get Sunshine and Boomer to the bridge to get us flying."

Boomer walked out of the room, heading to the bridge, while G.E.M. headed out to the engine room.

In the engine room, Victor was twisting a nut in a hard-to-reach place. His arm was stretched out with gears, belt, and piles surrounding it. "Careful…" He said with every twist of his wrench. "Careful…"

"Victor!" G.E.M.'s shout blasted into Victor's ear, frightening him and making him lose his grip on his wrench, dropping it.

G.E.M. stomped into the room. "Why are you stopping us from getting the Void out of here."

Victor jumped to his feet to face G.E.M. coming in with Pinky behind him. "I'm just trying to fix up the areas that I couldn't fix while in the air."

"We have dead Red Chains on the island with us," G.E.M. said, pointing his finger to the wall to reference outside. "We have no idea if there are any others, or if there are more coming to the island."

"Captain," Victor tried to address. "These areas I'm trying to fix up can't be worked on while in the air, without risking losing my limbs. Do you really want me to lose them? And if I don't fix them, there is no chance we'll survive Zone-X's winds."

G.E.M. shook his head, angrily unable to argue. "How much longer till we can finally get out of here."

"An hour." Victor told him, "If I can get my wrench."

"Make it so." G.E.M. orders, as the speakers start blaring.

"Captain!" Sunshine shouts through them. "Get to the bridge! Quick!"

G.E.M. and Pinky ran through halls of the ship, getting to the bridge. "What is it?" He questioned them.

"We just got a signal about a ship coming to the island." He explained.

"Please tell me it's not…" G.E.M. started to say.

"It's a Romeek ship." Sunshine told him, "But it's not showing a Red Chain signal."

"I told you not to tell me that!" G.E.M. shouted at him.

Chapter 15

Princess Zephyrus sat in one of the bedrooms, waiting for word about the Red Chains attacking the ship. She had just heard G.E.M.'s voice over the speak, but the loud cry for "Battle Stations!" made it clear that things were not going well.

'Did they board the ship?' Princess Zephyrus wondered. 'No. G.E.M.'s voice would not have appeared over the speaker if that was the case.'

Maybe Valen's forces had found them, or even more Red Chains were on their way, or maybe some massive monster was upon them.

Fear, or curiosity, got the better of her, and she headed out of the room to see what was going on. She went down the stairs to the bridge door, entering to see Sunshine at the controls.

"What's going on?" Princess Zephyrus asked, causing Sunshine to jump in his seat.

"Oh… Princess…." Sunshine addressed her, looking over his shoulder to see her. "Nothing big is happening. How about you go back upstairs and take a nap?"

Zephyrus knew something was up and stomped her foot. "I demand to know what is going on!" She shouted. "I am putting my life in your hands, and I don't want to be lied to about what is happening!"

Sunshine sighed, wondering just how bad she was going to take the news. "Okay," he told her. "We just found out that there were Red Chains on the island."

"Red Chains?" Zephyrus cried out. "They're the devils of the Romeek skies."

"Yeah," Sunshine told her. "Well, G.E.M. and the others just killed some of them, and now we have learned that a new Red Chains' ship has just appeared. Victor has not finished fixing the engine, and we can't take off till he does. So, our best bet is to try and hold them off till Victor can get us moving."

"What am I supposed to do in the mean time?" Zephyrus asked.

"I don't know. Hide in a chest or something?" Sunshine insulted her.

Zephyrus was angered by Sunshine's choice of words, storming out of the room to find G.E.M.

As she was storming down the hall, she felt something grab her by the shoulder of her dress and pull her into one of the rooms. When she got a moment to see who it was, she found May holding her tightly close to her.

"You need to stay here with me." May told her.

"Why is that?" Zephyrus shouted, not liking how May just pulled her aside without warning.

"Because we are not fighters." May told her. "Well… I can swing a mean frying pan, but other than that, we are not going to be able to do anything if we are invaded."

"So, we are going to be attacked by the Red Chains?" Zephyrus pointed out, with May just nodding in responds. "What if they do get in?" Zephyrus asked worried.

"Then pray they don't decide to kill us right away." May told her right to her face.

Zephyrus stayed quiet, wondering if the Red Chains would hear her if she made a peep.

"Get everyone into position!" G.E.M. shouted as he and his crew kneeled or stood behind crates, all aiming their guns at the opening. The ramp was lifted to be leveled with the floor, and to give the belly turret nearly 360-degree range around the ship.

G.E.M. and Pinky stayed on the right side, and Alan and Bob stayed on the left, waiting for their enemy to appear.

Tapping the earpiece in his ear, G.E.M. asked April and Boomer in the turret. "See anything?"

April was sitting in the lower turret with her hands on the triggers and her fingers hovering over the buttons. "I don't see anything at the moment. Maybe it was a false alarm."

"Red Chains are good at hiding." Pinky explained. "They are masters of surprise attacks."

"Only they use them mostly on the ground." G.E.M. pointed out. "Anything in the sky Boomer?"

There was no vocal response, but a small series of tiny and long beeps came through. It was code saying *No ship in sky.* Boomer was in his turret, pointing his gun and eyes towards the sky, and looking around for any sign of a ship.

"They aren't going to use their ship to attack?" Pinky asked.

"They might." G.E.M. said, "They mostly love getting blood on their shackles. Victor? Can you hurry. I would love to leave this place, before we're attacked."

"I might be able to cut some time, if I tape up some spots, but that's still fifteen minutes of work. And that still might get us killed later on." Victor warned.

"Do it." G.E.M. ordered. "I don't want to wait-" He was cut off by an arrow nearly hitting him but landing in the crate he was hiding behind instead. "They're here!"

Through the brown branches and green leaves, a massive group of muscular men in chains came charging towards the ship.

"We're going to die." Alan points out.

"I love you brother." Bob blurts out.

The numbers of the Red Chains grew. First ten, then twenty, then fifty, up to close to a hundred.

The four heard a blast from under the ship and an explosion that sent dirt, debris, and a few Red Chains into the air.

"Open fire!" G.E.M. ordered his crew while touching his communicator. "April! Try to thin down their numbers as much as possible. Keep them away from the legs. Boomer get down here and help us out."

All four of them opened fired on the charging army, aiming for any spots that didn't have chains around it. The head was the best place to aim, but with it being a small target compared to the chest, and the fact they were bobbing and weaving as they got closer made it hard to hit.

April sat in the turret cockpit, firing at anything that came towards the ship. The cannon fired over and over, having about two to three seconds between shots. Protecting the legs was her main order, but she also made sure to keep the Red Chains from reaching the opening the best she could.

"You will not hurt my Captain!" She shouted at the Red Chains, even though they could not hear her through the glass dome and the explosions.

The number of Red Chains was going down, but there were still too many of them.

Inside the cargo hold, Pinky shouted to her Captain. "Why are we leaving the cargo bay open?"

"I wanted to make sure we had a better chance of protecting the ship!" G.E.M. explained to her. "I worried that if we kept it closed, they would just attack us from all sides!"

"This is either the most brilliant or stupid plan you have ever had in your life." Pinky shouted, as a tomahawk whizzed past the right side of her face, barely missing her.

In the engine room, Victor was having a panic. "Come on! Come on! Come on!" He commanded the bolt he was currently fastening.

An explosion from somewhere outside the ship caused him to jump and toss his wrench in the air.

His wrench tumbled and spun in the air before Victor's eyes, but he reached out and was able to catch it.

"That was close." Victor told himself, getting back to work, worrying that at some point someone will come up from behind him and spilt his head open.

"They're getting closer!" Alan shouted, seeing some of the Red Chain starting to reach the hatch. An explosion close to it caused the ship to shake and make the four to fall on their butts.

Rushing back behind cover, before an arrow could hit him again, G.E.M. called out to April. "April! That was too close!"

"I'm sorry Captain." She called back, "But they just keep coming." The sound of glass shattering could be heard over the earbud.

"April!" He shouted, "Get out of there!"

There was no response, as a few Red Chains grabbed the hatch to lift themselves up. Luckily, they were quickly shot down as soon they poked their heads up.

"We're running out of bullets!" Pinky shouted, as she shot down another one trying to get on board.

Over by the lower turret, April had barely escaped, shutting the lid right on the head of a Red Chain.

"April?" May called out to her sister, causing her to look over at May poking her head out of the kitchen.

"Get back inside!" April ordered her little sister.

"But you can't keep that lid shut forever." May pointed out.

"I just need a little time." April told her.

"How much longer?" G.E.M. shouted over to Victor, before shooting a Red Chain in the exposed area around his heart and causing him to fall out of the ship.

"Just a little bit more." Victor said, wrapping some duct tape around some pipes. Once he felt it was done, he ripped the tape off with his teeth and shouted, "We're ready!"

"Sunshine!" G.E.M. commanded, "Get us the Void out of here!"

"Yes Captain!" Sunshine shouted, slamming down a lever to get the engines going. Wasting no time after that, Sunshine pulled the lever to pull the hatch back up and retract the landing legs back inside.

The Red Chains surrounded the ship, attacking the legs with axes, clubs, and swords, as the ship started to hover. Others tried one last chance to board by hanging on to the hatch. Those that did not slip off, lost their grip when their fingers were crushed by it closing.

Red Chains on the ground threw their spears, tomahawks, and arrows at the ship, before one shouted something, and they ran off.

"Where are they going?" Sunshine wondered aloud.

"What's happening?" G.E.M. asked him.

"They're going back the way they came." He spoke.

"They're going back to their ship." He realized, rushing down the hall to see April holding the lid of the turret shut.

"What's going on?" He asked.

"I've got some trapped in there." She said, struggling.

"May!" He shouted. "Block that thing with something heavy." He continued, reaching the bridge.

On the way, he contacted Boomer. "Boomer! Get back to the upper turret!"

Boomer signaled, *Already there.*

"Good. Sunshine fly the ship towards the way they're going and turn the Green-Eyed Monster on its side so Boomer can blast at their ship."

"Okay." Sunshine agreed, flying the ship the direction the Red Chains were going.

G.E.M. and Pinky got on the bridge, taking their spots. Meanwhile, Alan and Bob were fighting over the seat Boomer normally sat in.

The Green-Eyed Monster flew over the trees, reaching the edge of the island. Hovering over the edge, anchored down by the tree was a long ship covered with splats of red on it. It was oval shaped, with two massive wings, and one being used as a ramp.

The back end had a tail that was used for control.

"Turn the ship now!" G.E.M. ordered.

Sunshine turned the ship to its side. Alan and Bob fell onto the wall, having not buckled in time.

"Open fire!" G.E.M. shouted, and Boomer wasted no time bombarding the Red Chains' ship with rapid blasts.

The blast damaged the ship.

With that done, G.E.M. ordered, "Get us the Void out of here!" And the Green-Eyed Monster flew off and away from the Red Chains.

Chapter 16

After evading the Red Chain Pirates and flying for a couple hours, the crew was sitting around the dining table, eating some stew made from leftovers.

Boomer was the only one not there, as usual for him.

He may have liked staying for dinner, because no one was talking. The only sounds were slurps, gulps, and the constant banging from the belly turret that was sealed up with the heaviest chest they could find from their raid on the Leonardo.

Zephyrus sat there in the middle, looking around the table at everyone eyeing at their food. "Hmm…" She started to speak, "Are we going to do anything about the guy trapped on our ship?"

"How about he suffocates from the thin air?" G.E.M. answered, not looking up from his bowl. "But I think we wait three days and have him die from dehydration."

"You can't be serious!" Zephyrus shouted.

159

"Listen Princess," G.E.M. told her, "I'm sure someone of your stature knows that the Red Chains are barbaric fighters. They'll attack anyone and anything right away. And those chains they wear aren't for show…"

"I know." Zephyrus interrupted him, "They are from their imprisonment by the Romeek Empire. I also know that it was Badrick who freed the first Red Chains when he broke out of his shackles and slaughtered the entire Romeek crew that was transporting him."

G.E.M. and Zephyrus glared at each other, causing the rest of the crew at the table to stop eating and stare back and forth between the two.

"Okay…" Pinky broke the dreading quiet and clapped her hands together. "I think I had enough. Whoever wants my bowl can have it. Princess Zephyrus, would you kindly come with me?"

Zephyrus was about to ask why but having stayed on the Green-Eyed Monster long enough to realize that it was a bad idea to stay and argue with

G.E.M. Getting up, she and Pinky left the kitchen and dining area.

As they left, the rest of the crew looked over at G.E.M., who just looked at them and got back to his food.

He ate three spoonful bites before asking Victor. "Do you think you can fix the engine enough to get us through the Zone-X storm?" He did not look up from his bowl.

Victor flinched for a second, before replying. "Maybe… I had to rush through most of the repairs, but there could be a chance for us surviving, if we get through it the first round."

G.E.M. looked up from his bowl directly at Victor. "And if we don't?"

"Then the engines might explode, or die on us, killing all of us shortly after that." Victor nervously explained.

"That's just great." G.E.M. tossed his spoon into the stew, making it splash. "What did I do to deserve this fate?" Alan and Bob were about to answer, but G.E.M. quickly cut them off with his words and his guns. "Don't answer that!"

"What do you want us to do in the meantime?" May asked.

"We should continue doing our normal routines on the ship," G.E.M. explained, "But we're going to have to be extra vigilante. Not only do we have the Valen after us, but I'm sure Badrick is going to get word about us killing a bunch of his men. I'm not even sure the Zone-X vow of peace is going to stop him and his crew from coming after us if we make it."

Everyone at the table looked over at G.E.M. nodding. "Well," April got up. "I'm full. How about I take you back to the med bay and check out that wound?"

G.E.M. looked down at his bandaged stomach, having forgotten about it after the fight. Looking up at April's wicked smile, he quickly told her. "No. I'm fine. There's no need."

"But we need to change your bandages, and I have to make sure that wound is not infected." April argued.

"Are you going to need to…" G.E.M. gulped, "cut me open?"

"Maybe…" April said, smiling at the idea.

G.E.M. start panicking, as April walked over, grabbed him by the collar of his jacket, and dragged him out of the dining area kicking and screaming for help.

"Does anyone want to save him?" Victor asked, with everyone else shaking their heads or saying 'no'.

Zephyrus and Pinky made it up to Pinky's quarters, with Zephyrus still mad. "I can't believe how heartless he is!" She shouted, "He's worse than anything I ever heard."

"I will admit that he doesn't act like the most 'caring' person, but he does what he does for us." Pinky explained.

"You mean for you and your crewmates."
Zephyrus pointed out to her, "The only reason I'm not falling to my death, is because it would be too much 'trouble' for him."

"Well… I can't argue with you there." She admitted, "But G.E.M. is a pretty okay guy. I met him when he just became captain, and he was looking for some new crewmembers to replace those that were leaving."

"Just how long has G.E.M. been leading the Green Coats?" Zephyrus asked. "He doesn't look like someone who's been around for decades."

"That… I can't tell you." Pinky told her. "But I can tell you how we first met."

Zephyrus sat on the bed. "Okay."

Pinky sat in a nearby chair. "My father was from the Buscadores de Oro."

"The Gold Seekers." Zephyrus interrupted.

"Yes." Pinky nodded, "My mother was a house wife. We did make a good living, thanks to my father's… 'job' with the small fleet."

"What did he do?" Zephyrus asked, "Was he just a regular pirate?"

"That wouldn't have paid for the life I had." Pinky explained. "He was the captain of one of the ships, the Estrella Dorada. I wanted to join him on his ship, but he didn't want me to become a Buscadores de Oro."

"So how did you and him meet?" Zephyrus asked.

"It was about six years ago that I first meet Captain G.E.M." Pinky told her.

Chapter 17

My family were not nobles, but were high class, like Sunshine, but that's his story. My mother was your everyday housewife. Mostly sitting around drinking tea or wine, playing games with her fellow housewife friends, or just sitting around, while servants took care of the house.

My father, as I stated, was a privateer with the Buscadores de Oro and captain of the Estrella Dorada. He was good at his job and provided more for us than we knew what to do with. But that also meant that he was hardly ever home, if he even wanted to come home at all.

I was, and still am, a smart girl. I had private tutors when it came to my education and professional trainers for anything I could ask for. Horseback riding, swimming, fighting, sword fighting, and shooting. I loved getting the chance to use a gun when I could, even though it was frowned upon by some.

My mother honestly did not care what I did with my life, so I was free to do anything I wanted. That was how I was able to do all those things.

When, and if, my father was ever home, I would have him tell me about his plundering and adventures.

It was like a wonderful dream every time I got to hear him talk about it. He made each attack seem like an epic story, instead of a bloody massacre like I'm sure it truly was. I remember one such time.

"We were lying in wait for a ship filled with gold to come our way." He explained, "The crew and I keep the engines low to not give away our position."

"As we waited, we made sure to follow the sun to hide our ships presence."

"Then… they came. A large vessel. Larger than any I had ever seen in all my years. It had to be a hundred feet long and fifty feet tall. It was a beauty unlike any other."

"As soon as it was in range, we attacked, firing all our cannons at it, before they had the chance to counter. We aimed for their weapons first, making sure their chances to defeat us lessened."

"We took some damage, but it was nothing compared to what we did to them. We knew how to straighten our ship when they fired and attack their broad side when we could."

"Once we had them on the ropes, we flew our ship over their heads, dropped out of the sky like lightening, and boarded their ship."

"Despite our earlier attacks, they were still able to put up a tough fight. I had five, no six men on me at the same time. But they were no match for me, as I cut them all down with one swing."

"The captain was a tough opponent. We fought all over his bedchambers, throwing everything within reach at each other, using all the furniture to defend ourselves from the other's blade. But in the end, I cut off both his hands and dragged him out before his crew to make them surrender. We took all the gold our ship could carry. We had to decide who would be left behind so we could sail out with the spoils."

"We made sure to contact one of the other ships in the fleet, and those that wished to join us were given the right. Those that didn't... went to see their families again."

Now I believe that was a lie, and he killed them.

I can see you're shocked by this, just as I was when I came to that realization.

When I got older, I asked my father to vouch for me to join the Buscadores de Oro, but he wouldn't hear of it. Instead, he planned on marrying me off to some noble's son.

I wasn't excited about this, and my excitement lessened the moment I laid eyes on my intended husband.

I decided to run away that day and boarded a ship heading out. I dyed my hair, changed my name, and changed my clothing too. It took me a little while, but my skills allowed me to make my way to Zone-X. There, I began looking for work. Most of the places wanted to just hire me for sex rather than for my skills.

A few days later, I finally ran into G.E.M. looking for new crewmembers. It went a little something like this.

"What kind of crew members are you looking for?" I asked him.

"What can you do?" He asked me with a smile.

I didn't answer him right away. I decided to show him by pulling out my pistol and firing it a few times.

You should have seen the look on his face. I wish I had a picture of it to hang on a wall for all to see.

"What's your name?" He asked me after that.

"Pinky." I told him.

"That's one weird name."

"Well, what is your name?" I asked him.

"I am G.E.M. The Green-Eyed Monster." He proudly said.

"Well, G.E.M. is a weird name as well."

We talked it over for a while, and he learned that I was the daughter of a Buscadores de Oro captain, he agreed to make me his first mate. That's how I met Boomer and Victor as well.

My family… They soon learned about me joining the Green Coats during a meeting of the seven captains. My father was pissed when he saw me standing next to G.E.M.

That was the moment that G.E.M. learned my real name. He had promised not to tell anyone and would continue calling me Pinky if I wished.

I told him that I did, and he responded to my father by saying, "I do not know who this woman you think my first mate is. This is Pinky. My right-hand woman, first mate of the Green Coats, and the one I trust with my life above all others. I am sorry for the confusion sir."

My father was livid after that, but it turned out all right in the end.

And that is how I first meet G.E.M.

Chapter 18

It had been two days after the run in with Red Chains. In that time, the banging from the belly turret had finally stopped. At worse the Red Chain inside had given up and was hoping someone would open the hatch, and at best had fallen out of the turret and was now falling endlessly into the Void.

In the holding bay, G.E.M. was shouting orders. "Tie those things down tight! I don't want to risk them getting any more damaged than they might already be!" He was wearing his normal clothing, and still had his stomach area wrapped up in bandages.

Alan and Bob were yanking down on the rope they were currently holding, trying to tie down one of the last crates they had.

"What's going on here?" Zephyrus asked, getting G.E.M.'s attention.

Turning around to see her standing in the hallway, he told her. "We will be reaching Zone-X soon, and we need to make sure everything is fastened and tied down, or otherwise things will be going flying all over the place. If that happens, the ship could get damaged and get us killed."

Zephyrus nodded, understanding what he was saying. "Is there anything I can do?"

G.E.M. looked at her, stopping to think it over. "How about you go to the bridge and get the weather report from Boomer?"

"Okay." Zephyrus said, heading off. As she walked down the hall, she noticed April in the med bay, seemingly to be getting ready as well.

Zephyrus watched, as April hummed, putting all the supplies she had out into drawers, cabinets, and closets. The ship's doctor used a key to unlock the drawers. Once she had it filled, she would close and lock it back up.

She did not say anything, continuing down the hall to see May doing the same thing in the kitchen.

Just like her big sister, she hummed around the kitchen and dining areas. There was a bit more of a pep in her step and a smile on her face as she got ready for Zone-X's hurricane force winds.

Continuing, Zephyrus came across the hatch that currently housed the Red Chain. Zephyrus stared at it, imagining the barbarian popping out of the turret like some monster swinging his ax.

'Did he have an ax?' She thought to herself. She did not want to ever know and kept on going.

When she got to the bridge, Zephyrus saw Pinky and Sunshine at their seats near the controls. Boomer was at his station, getting the weather report for the rest of the crew.

Pinky turned her head when she heard the door open, excepting G.E.M., when she saw Zephyrus, she smiled but was a little confused.

"Hello Zephyrus," Pinky greeted, "What brings you here today?"

"I was bored." Zephyrus semi-admitted, "I wanted to help, and G.E.M. sent me here to get the weather report from Boomer."

"Okay." Pinky nodded, "It will be smooth sailing for the most part, but I don't want to fly into a thunder cloud before we get to Zone-X."

"Aren't we going to be flying through gale force winds when going through Zone-X?" Sunshine pointed out to her. "Those are worse than any thunder cloud. And with Victor not being able to fix up the engine like he wanted..." He stopped himself, not wanting to say another word.

Pinky did not respond, nor did Zephyrus. Boomer got up from his seat, walked over to Zephyrus, and handed her a piece of paper.

Zephyrus looked down at it. It read, "Wind picking up. Getting close. Nothing else to report."

Zephyrus looked up at Boomer's covered head. "Thanks." She told him, "I will get this to G.E.M."

Boomer nodded, heading back to his seat. Zephyrus walked out, heading back to the storage area.

When she got back, she saw G.E.M. helping Alan and Bob with tying down the last of their stolen goods.

He pulled on some rope with Alan and Bob, securing one of the larger crates in place.

Zephyrus kindly just stood there, waiting and watching.

Looking over at the hallway entrance, G.E.M. saw Zephyrus standing there watching. He let go of the rope, without warning Alan and Bob, and they were sling-shot face first into a massive crate.

"What did Boomer say about the weather?" G.E.M. asked the princess.

Zephyrus handed G.E.M. the paper Boomer gave her, and he looked it over.

"Hm…" G.E.M. noted, "Looks like it's clear sailing for us." He said, as Alan and Bob struggled on the rope.

"That's… great…" Alan struggled out.

"A little… help… Captain…" Bob asked.

G.E.M. looked over, rushing back to help the gunner brothers.

Victor was currently in the engine room, looking at the red-hot engine. His goggles covered his eyes, that would have dried out if he did not have them on, or maybe the sweat he was pouring from his forehead would have keep them moist.

He held out his shaky, gloved hands at the engine, as if trying to make it heal.

The engine grinded and pumped, the gyro sphere spun wildly.

"This is not good." Victor commented, looking over the engine for anything that could help it. He saw some piping that looked like it was building up too much pressure.

"I need to release some of the pressure." Victor spoke, reaching for his wrench, and rushing over. It took a few turns, and with one last turn Victor stepped back.

He got to work finding a safe spot along the engine and stepped aside to let the heat and steam out. "There." He said, wiping his sweating forehead.

"Lunch is ready!" May's voice rang from the speakers, causing Victor to freeze up and drop his wrench.

Once he was able to unfreeze, he picked up his wrench. "I freakin' hate that!"

It was mostly the same as it has been for the past few days, with Victor still not there, Boomer getting his food to eat by himself, and Zephyrus joining the rest of the crew at the table.

Everyone was eating the randomized stew again, slurping the soupy part and chewing the chunky bits.

Looking up in from his bowl, G.E.M. addressed the crew. "We will soon be reaching the storm of Zone-X. Alan, Bob, and I got the crates tied down. Does everyone else have everything ready?"

"I got my room and office cleaned up." April told her captain first. "Everything is where it should be, and the drawers and cabinets are locked up to keep them from falling out."

"Once we finish eating, I will clean the dishes and put them back up." May spoke up next.

"Sunshine and I checked the rooms to make sure everyone had their stuff put away." Pinky chimed in next. "That just leaves your room for you to do sir."

"Alright." He nodded in response, before looking over at Zephyrus. "Once we're safely through the storm and on the island, I'll hand you over to the old man."

Zephyrus looked from her still full bowl, staring at him. "Then what?"

"Then you are out of our hair, the Zǐ Sè Dēng Pào smuggle you into Hǔ Bǎi Hé and show you to the officials, we are no longer blamed for your 'death', and you get sanctuary and an army to help you get your kingdom back."

Zephyrus stared at G.E.M., seeming to be deciding to either thank him or insult him.

Everyone else stayed quiet, not wanting to get involved by any means.

A buzz came over the speakers in Morse code.

Everyone looked up, focusing on the sounds coming through. Their eyes started to widen as the message was sent.

"What is it?" Zephyrus asked, not knowing what was going on.

"Boomer is telling us…" G.E.M. said, letting the message sink in. "We are closing in on Zone-X!" He shot out of his chair, surprising everyone. "Green Coats! Battle Stations on the double!"

Everyone shot up from their seats, except Zephyrus. Only she and Alan were left in the dining area with May, who was rushing to clean up, and G.E.M., wondering what they were waiting for.

"Hm…" Alan spoke, "Where am I supposed to go? The belly glass protecting the belly turret is broken, and their still might be a Red Chain in here."

"Go join your brother in the upper turret." G.E.M. told him. "And make sure he knows that that's an order."

Alan nodded and headed off.

"And as for you," he said directly at Zephyrus, "Come with me. You are about to get your first, and maybe last, look at the storm of Zone-X."

Chapter 19

Princess Zephyrus stood next to G.E.M. as they looked out the ship's window.

"No matter how many times I see it," G.E.M. told Princess Zephyrus, "it still terrifies and leaves me in awe."

The Princess looked out at the storm that raged and swirled aggressively. "I heard that it has never stopped from the moment it was first founded centuries ago and was still raging before then." She told them.

"You are not wrong Princess." G.E.M. agreed, "You can see what remains of those foolish enough to try and fly through the storm without knowing how." He pointed out of the windshield at the storm, and just as he said there were the remains of ships, pieces of cargo, and if they looked closely, there were even the bodies of the dead forever trapped in Zone-X's winds.

"How in God's name do you intend to get through?" Princess Zephyrus asked G.E.M., finding it impossible.

"I told you." He said, "We are not going through it, but only have to get to the eye of the storm."

"And how do you plan on doing that?"

G.E.M. over at Victor sitting close by. "Victor," he asked. "How does the engine look?"

"I did all I could with what I had." He told him. "But we may have only one chance."

"Isn't that how it always works?" G.E.M. grinned at the challenge.

"Not like this." Victor told him, "The engines are still pretty beat up from that Valen attack, and the attack from the Red Chains didn't help either. If we do not make it through the storm, we will not just be trapped for a little while till we sort ourselves out, we will be trapped forever. Which in turn will cause our ship to get ripped to shreds and kill all of us."

"What is he talking about?" Princess Zephyrus asked them.

G.E.M. glared at the princess. "Victor, would you mind explaining for our 'guest'?"

Victor looked over at the princess, kneeling to her level. "You see… most times, when a ship misses it chance to 'turn' in the storm, we'd have to wait till it comes up again; or fly themselves out right away.

"Turn in the storm?" Zephyrus questioned Victor's choice of wording.

"It is more complicated than that," He explained, "but we sadly cannot show you."

"Why is that?" She asked.

"If all the crews that use Zone-X as a hideout learned you saw how to get in, they will kill you right away, then they will execute all of us for just bringing you there." G.E.M. told her "They'll fear that if you get back, you will tell the Valen armada how to get through the storm, and they will attack our safe haven. Void, they may just kill us all anyway if they see you."

Zephyrus gulped, not knowing what was worse. The raging storm that stood before them, or the murderous pirates that awaited inside. "But it will not be possible to see through the storm?" She realized, "With it raging the way it does, there is no way I would be able to tell how to get through."

"We cannot take that chance." G.E.M. told her.

"But there may be a way you could stay here with us, while we fly in." Pinky walked up, showing Zephyrus a long rag.

"Blindfold?" G.E.M. pondered.

"It's too dangerous for her to be any of the rooms," Pinky explained. "This way, we can keep her safe in here with the rest of us, and she does not see the path."

G.E.M sighed, "Okay. But be sure to tie her arms behind her and on one of the railings. I do not want to give her the chance of taking it off if she thinks about it."

"Okay Captain." Pinky agreed, taking Princess Zephyrus by the hand, and leading her along.

"Now that we have that done," G.E.M. turned this attention to the rest of the crew.

"Boomer, we are counting on you to tell us when and where to go."

Boomer just gave him a thumbs-up.

"Sunshine, you and Pinky are going to have to keep your grip tight while we're flying through."

"Aye aye Captain." Sunshine saluted him.

"Alan! Bob!" G.E.M. called out to them over the intercom, "I am counting on the both of you to protect the ship from any debris that comes our way. We're going to be blind under our belly, with the turret out of action."

"You got it Captain!" They both called back.

G.E.M. turned to look over at May and April, who were both sitting in their seats and already buckled in. May was clearly scared, fearing the Zone-X storm, but April smiled at G.E.M. licking the scalpel she always carried with her.

G.E.M. shivered at the sight of what April was doing, before turning to get in his seat. Buckling himself in for safely, he addressed the crew. "Everyone buckle-up, this is going to be an all or nothing shot. If we miss this, we are all dead.

So, I am going to ask all of you this one more time, and I better hear the truth. Are we all ready?"

Boomer gave another thumbs-up, Alan and Bob called in, Sunshine gripped the controls, Victor took his seat,

Pinky finished tying, and blindfolding, the princess up tight to one of the railings so she would not get thrown around the ship. Getting her seat, she bucked in. "Ready!"

"Then let us go!" G.E.M. shouted as they flew into the massive storm.

The ship blasted off at full speed right into the winds. Right away the ship was pulled by the storm, keeping it from going straight. Everyone was thrown sideways, just as they told the princess. If none of them were buckled in, they would have been thrown against the walls of the bridge.

"This is worse than I originally thought!" Victor shouted over the howling storm. "The engines are getting ripped apart by Zone-X's hurricane winds!"

"Then we better not waste a single second!" G.E.M. shouted back at him, before turning to Pinky and Sunshine. "Start pushing us…" He waited for the right moment. "NOW!"

Pinky and Sunshine slammed on the accelerators, causing them to fly forward a bit, before they stopped.

"What is happening?" Princess Zephyrus called out, still blindfolded and tied to the railing.

"Hit the acceleration again!" G.E.M. ordered right away, ignoring Princess Zephyrus's question.

Pinky and Sunshine followed their captain's orders, pushing a bit farther into the storm.

Just then, a large explosion was heard from the back of the ship. "We are starting to lose the engines!" Victor shouted.

To make matters worse, the Green-Eyed Monster started to spin and lean over to its right side.

"Damn it!" G.E.M. shouted, "We have to try and get that engine back on line! Or we are all screwed!"

"The only way to do that would be to go into the engine room and repair it manually!" Victor told them, "And I will not be able to reach it while we are like this!"

"Pinky! Sunshine! Boomer! I need you three to do what you can to straighten the ship up enough for Victor!" G.E.M. shouted at his crew, before remembering about Alan and Bob. "Alan! Bob!" He called them over the income, "I need you two to start firing guns when I give the order! Point your gun to your right!"

"Aye aye Captain!" They all, but Boomer, shouted back to him.

"Do it now!" G.E.M. shouted, as they went through with the plan.

Right away Pinky and Sunshine started turning the controls to straighten the ship, while Alan and Bob started firing to help turn the ship straight again.

The winds fought back, making the crew struggle against its power.

The struggle was not helping the ship, as Victor pointed out that the harder they fought, the more strain it put on their last engine.

"You are probably going to have get to the engines than!" G.E.M. shouted over to him, "We will keep trying to straighten the ship, and get us to the eye of the storm!"

"I..." Victor thought about arguing with his captain but looking into G.E.M.'s eyes showed they were dead if he did not go now. "I will do what I can Captain!"

"Then go now!" He ordered, waving his arm towards the door.

Victor nodded, carefully unbuckling his belt. Because his seat was on the left side of the ship, he had to carefully get out, holding on to his chair as he moved.

Holding on to the head of the chair, Victor slightly hung over G.E.M., and dropped down. He was able to land on G.E.M.'s seat, nearly bumping into his captain.

"Sorry Captain." He apologized.

"Apologize when we are not about to die."
G.E.M. told him, "Now go!"

Victor nodded, looking over at the doorway. Using all his strength, he jumped towards it, getting about half way through.

"What are you guys doing?" G.E.M. turned his attention to the rest of the crew, "get this ship straighten up!"

"Yes Captain!" They shouted in response, as Victor pushed and pulled his way through to the other side of the door.

"Any ideas on what we should do Boomer?" Pinky called out to their navigator.

Boomer studied the radar screen and signed them on what they should do.

"Okay Boomer, we are trusting you!"

Boomer just nodded, signing Pinky and Sunshine the entire time.

As the winds continued pushing against the ship, the crew used as little power as possible to continue. This proved to be a losing battle, as without both engines, the ship had no chance in the storm.

"We are not going to make it!" Pinky shouted.

"Victor?" G.E.M. called over the speakers, "Please tell me you are about to be finished with fixing the engines in ten seconds!"

There was no response on the other end. The whole crew's worry got worse as the silence answered back.

"What is going on?" Zephyrus called out, fighting to free herself so she could remove the blindfold. The crew panicking, the storm raging; all it was doing was causing her imagination to create a world of death and doom in the darkness she was being forced to just listen.

G.E.M. was starting to wonder if they were all doomed as well. That he and his crew would be trapped in the Zone-X storm for the all eternity. Their ship would be seen by other sky pirates of present and future, as the fools who did not follow the path.

They were about to accept their fate, when Victor finally came over the speaker. "I am here Captain!" He shouted over the speaker, "I am working on the engine! We do not have much time! I will have to work on it while it is running!"

"Are you sure?" G.E.M. asked him.

"We have no choice!" Victor told him, "It is either this, or we die."

G.E.M. looked at the rest of the crew on the bridge, having only a short time to decide. "Do it." He told them.

They all nodded but turned the engine back on.

The crew felt the engine running, but as they thought it was not enough to push them as much as they needed.

"We are not going to make it!" Pinky shouted.

"Victor!" G.E.M. shouted, "Please tell me you got those engines working to full power!"

"I can't Captain!" He called back, "I can only get them fixed so much."

"We are going to be trapped in the Zone-X storm forever!" Sunshine shouted.

Zephyrus' panic was too much for her to bare, breaking down, and crying.

G.E.M. truly felt this was the end of him and the Green Coats. How were they going to get out of this one?

The ship twisted, spun, and turned in the storm, causing the Green Coats to lose themselves. Everything was going by so fast; it was nothing but a blur to them. Even Boomer's radar could not read anything.

"I'm sorry crew." G.E.M. told them. "I've failed you."

Just then the power started coming back, helping the ship against the winds.

The speaker came on, and Victor's voice could be heard shouting from it, "I got the engine back up and running! But it's still barely holding! If we don't make it now, we won't get a third chance!"

G.E.M looked at the rest of his crew. "You heard the man! Get us out of this Void storm!"

"Yes Captain!" Pinky and Sunshine shouted, not looking back at him, but forward into the storm.

They stepped on the gas and blasted forward.

As they were pushing their way through, a large piece of debris came its way.

"Oh no you don't!" Alan fired his cannon at the debris, destroying it before it could reach them.

"Nice shot!" Bob commented.

"There's still more on the way!" Alan told him, as he fired at more things that got close.

"How much longer!" G.E.M. shouted, hoping to see some light at the end of the storm tunnel.

No one answered him, all focusing on getting the ship out of the storm before they blew up or worse.

Just then, something came up on Boomer radar, and he signaled for the captain.

"What is it?" He asked, "Are we close?"

Boomer nodded.

"Then point the way!" G.E.M. yelled, "Let's reach Teach Island!"

"Teach Island?" Zephyrus repeated to herself out of confusion.

The Green-Eyed Monster pushed and pulled against the howling winds of Zone-X, fighting with all its might. The engines fought with all the energy they had left. The cannon blasted away anything that threatened the ship.

Inside the bridge, Pinky noticed a faint light. "There!" She shouted. "There's the way out!"

"Well let's not waste any more time!" G.E.M. shouted, "Let's get out of here!"

Pinky and Sunshine shouted at the top of their lungs in some belief it would push the ship harder.

Strangely it did seem to work, causing the ship to push past the winds ahead to go straight for the light.

In the engine room, Victor saw how the stress was affecting the engine. "Captain!" He called, "We need to hurry! The engine seems to be about to blow!"

"Just a little further!" G.E.M told him, hoping they would make it.

The light grew larger and larger, till it finally glowed around them all.

All the while Zephyrus was looking around the room, with nothing but a blindfold of darkness all around her. "What is it? Did we make it? Are we alive?" She continuously asked, till the blindfold was pulled away.

"Welcome to Teach Island." G.E.M. told her, "We hope you enjoy the view."

Zephyrus looked out of the ship in awe at the sight before her eyes.

Chapter 20

The crew looked at the island that floated in the center of Zone-X's monstrous storm. Unlike the storm that raged around it, the island was bathed in the beauty of the sunlight that came from the hole overhead in the clouds. It was like an oasis in the desert after the trouble they had been through.

G.E.M. stood. "There it is." He pointed out the windshield to the island in front of them. There was a massive mountain in the background that caught her eyes first. The broken ground under it made it appear as though the entire island was in a bowl.

"What is that mountain?" Zephyrus pointed to the peak, after G.E.M. untied her arms.

"That is Mt. Teach. Named after Captain Teach of the Sky Devils." He explained to her. "They were the first to traverse the storm and they found this island. This allowed them to attack ships and then escape with no way for their enemies to follow them."

"After his death, most of his crew formed their own crews, and used their knowledge of the storm to turn this into a safe haven for all pirates."

Princess Zephyrus looked in awe, as her attention turned to the city that was located next to the docks. There were dozens of ships of different shapes and sizes, many of them had the same design. Those ships were clearly part of the same fleets.

"Good news Captain," Pinky addressed him, "there are the Zǐ Sè Dēng Pào's ships."

The crew looked out to see them. They were designed with two Hǔ Bǎi Hé dragons on each side, seeming to be carrying the ship between them. On the mid-back was a small tower that was surrounded by cannons on all sides. On the top of the tower was the flag of the Zǐ Sè Dēng Pào, an un-bloomed flower bud inside a circle.

"I learned about those ships." Princess Zephyrus said, "The dragons are said to be the great protectors of the empire, and the tower is where the most powerful members watch over the rest."

"Smart girl," Sunshine commented.

"Indeed." G.E.M. just stared down at her, not caring one bit about the history lesson she just gave. "Sunshine! Signal the docks that we are coming in for a landing! Boomer! Find us an open docking station! I don't what to spend another second in this can of death."

Boomer and Sunshine looked over their shoulders at G.E.M., nodding. They were able to find a spot near the far west end of the docks.

With Sunshine letting them know they were coming; dockhands were there to help hook them from the outside.

Once they locked in, G.E.M. called the crew over to the storage area to assign them their duties while there.

"Our mission is to find Izanagi of the Zǐ Sè Dēng Pào and hand Princess Zephyrus over to him." He went over to stand with them. "Boomer, Alan, Victor, Sunshine, and I will be heading into town. Victor is going to take Sunshine to get supplies to repair the ship, not to mention replenish any food and water supplies that we will need when we leave. Boomer, Alan, and I are going to visit Izanagi and bring him here to get you Princess Zephyrus." He finished speaking by looking directly at her.

"Are you sure he can be trusted?" She asked him.

"Izanagi is a loyal follower of Hǔ Bǎi Hé and the strongly practitioner of Shèng Kāi De Huā Duǒ." G.E.M. explained to her. "If there is one thing that keeps him from completely freeing his soul, it is all the plundering and fighting he does to protect his homeland. Which brings me to the rest of you!" He turned back towards his crew, "April, May, Pinky, Bob will stay here to protect the Princess and the ship till we get back with Izanagi. Victor and Sunlight will be sure to help you if they get here before Boomer, Alan, and me."

"Yes Captain." Pinky nodded.

G.E.M. nodded back to her, turning around to head to the tail end of the ship. "Princess Zephyrus," he addressed her, "Please go deep inside the ship, so no one sees you."

"Why?" She questions.

"Cause..." He tells her, "If someone sees you, our lives will be in danger if they do. I thought I explained this to you earlier."

Princess Zephyrus stayed quiet, nodded in agreement, and walked away down the ship's hall. The five waited, as G.E.M. pressed a button. The hanger bay door started to lower, becoming a ramp for the Green Coats.

As they walked down, G.E.M. was greeted by some of the people on the docks. "Greetings Captain G.E.M.," they greeted, nodding their heads as if to bow. "The usual?"

"What do you think? Get the Void away from our ship, or I'll slaughter the all of ya!" He barked at them, causing them to run off.

With them gone, G.E.M. turned back to the rest of the crew that were still on the ship, watching the hanger bay door close again. "Keep the ship safe." He told them, with Pinky just nodding at his orders.

When the door closed, Pinky turned towards the remaining crew, giving them orders right away. "Okay guys, we've got to make sure no one tries to get on board while we are here; and if they do, they don't leave here alive."

"Yes ma'am!" They all shouted.

"Bob," Pinky addressed him first. "You will watch the hanger door."

"You got it!" He smiled, walking up past her, standing near the door.

"May," Pinky addressed her next. "How about you make us something to eat? We can't guard the ship on an empty stomach."

"I will see what we have left in the kitchen, but I can't promise it will be much." She explained, "We did have that big party. Not to mention all the food we lost from the attack back in Valen."

"Just see what you can do. We could all use a little snack after all we've been through." Pinky told her, before looking at the last crew member left to do something. "April can you..."

"Watch the doors? I will do that." April interrupted her, giving a charming smile.

"Hmm… okay…" Pinky just stared.

"So, what are you going to do?" April asked Pinky.

"I am going to watch the Princess till G.E.M. and the others get back." Pinky explained to the crew.

While that was going on, Victor and Sunshine were arguing with a merchant over some parts. "You are hacking up the god damn prices!" Victor shouted at the seller on the other side of the desk.

"It is not my fault." The seller calmly told him, "It is getting harder to get parts in here with Valen hunting down all pirates ever since their Princess was killed."

Victor just gritted, learning what had been happening because of them. "Fine. I will just keep looking." He walked away with Sunshine.

"You don't have to yell at him like that." Sunshine told his friend, as they kept walking.

"We are freakin' stuck here, and till I get our engines fixed, we are going to continue to be stuck here." Victor complained, pissed off.

As they were walking, Sunshine looked around, before leaning in close to whisper to Victor. "Do you think what he said was true? Cause if it is…"

"Who knows?" Victor whispered back, shrugging his shoulders. "But yeah… I understand what you're getting at."

"Okay." Sunshine nodded, as the two continued looking for parts.

Over with G.E.M., Alan, and Boomer were busy making their way through the street and alleys. They ran into some children that were playing between the buildings. Children of pirates that were born and raised on the island, with no idea about what was on the other side of the maelstrom, besides the stories they would overhear from those that had returned.

There were a few prostitutes working the walkways, trying to call G.E.M. and his men over to them. G.E.M. had no problems with the fine ladies of the night, but he had business to do before he could enjoy any pleasures. There were a few moments where G.E.M. or Boomer had to either drag Alan away, or just bop him on the head to get him back in line.

They saw other pirates walking along, gambling, or drunk. It was easy to avoid them, as no one would want to start a fight where everyone had a gun or blade hidden on their body.

The three reached a two-story tall build that had foreign writing on the sign. The walls were painted red, with brown shingles on the roofs. The first-floor windows were circular, and covered with paper to avoid any peeking. The second floor had balconies, with sliding paper doors to allow guests to go outside, but it was unlikely anyone would want to.

The smell of sex and alcohol filling his nose caused him to step back. "What the Void!" He stated, covering his nose from the smell. "What happened here?"

He looked at the building more, feeling, and smelling something completely different about the place.

"Why would the old man turn this into a whorehouse?" He asked himself. "That's not like him."

The trio wasted no time going in, where they were greeted by a beautiful Hu Bia He woman that wore a loose-fitting kimono. "How may I help you young gentlemen today?" She asked them with a welcoming smile.

"We're here to meet Izanagi." G.E.M. told her.

"Alright," She nodded, handing him a tag. "She will meet you in the private chambers."

"She?" G.E.M. repeated.

"Yes." The hostess nodded, "She will explain everything."

G.EM. did not like this, looking and stepping around, as if planning for an escape route.

Alan and Boomer looked at their captain, wondering what was going on with him.

"Um… thanks." He told the hostess, as he commanded the other two to follow him.

As they walked past some of the rooms, moans and cries could be heard coming from within a few of them. Shadows of employees and customers could be seen on the paper walls and doors, giving Alan and Boomer an idea of what was going on behind them.

G.E.M. did not pay any attention to the other people in the place, as he was already filled with questions. 'What did she mean by 'she'?' He pondered, 'What happened to Izanagi? I thought we saw his ship when we first got here. Could I have been mistaken?'

The trio climbed up the stairs to the second floor, as they continued their way to the far end of the building.

They spotted three guards blocking a double set door. Two of them Hǔ Bǎi Hé women, wearing tightly tied kimonos. Their faces were stern, staring ahead at the three as they walked forward, while the two gripped the dual katana kept by their sides.

The third was a large man in a brown vest to show off his muscular chest and arms. Both his hands had brass knuckles, which he showed off by cracking his knuckles.

G.E.M. and Boomer were not worried. Alan was a little freaked out by the large man that looked like he could crush his skull like a grape. G.E.M. shoved the tag right in front of the guards' faces, making it clear he did not have time for their crap.

"I've got to speak with your boss." He told them. "Now get the Void out of my way."

The large guard took the tag, staring at it, before stepping aside and bowing.

G.E.M.'s face stayed firm, as they walked up to the large sliding doors and forced them opened.

The inter room was pentagon shaped, with red walls and a pillar in each corner. The hard wood floor had a pentagon design on it, with each corner of the design touching the center of each wall. This pattern repeated inside each other, until it disappeared under a large rug.

The rug was not of Hǔ Bǎi Hé design. Their rugs were made with images of great breasts like tigers, dragons, or falcons. The rug had an Al-Hawabic design with patters and shapes.

In the center of the rug was a traditional Hǔ Bǎi Hé table, with two pillows on each side.

Beyond that, was a desk, with two chairs in front of it. But it was the one sitting at the desk that shocked G.E.M. the most.

He was expecting Izanagi. An old, yet strong man that did not need to demand respect but did so to make sure no one challenged him.

But instead was a gorgeous woman with silk black hair that went down to her jaw line, and piercing brown eyes. One leg resting on top of the table, with the lower half of her loose-fitting red kimono riding up almost past her thigh. The kimono had a crane design that went up to her chest area, showing off a good amount of cleavage to the three.

One hand held a long smoking pipe that she puffed, while the other hand flipped through some paperwork. She looked up at the three, smiling. "It's been a long time, hasn't it G.E.M.?" She said, taking her leg off the desk to sit properly.

"Hello Izanami," G.E.M. greeted back at her. "What are you doing here?"

"I own this building." She said, "It is the property of Zǐ Sè Dēng Pào."

"I mean, what happened to Izanagi? Where is he?" G.E.M. seeming demanded, causing the three guards to start coming to their leader's defenses.

Boomer and Alan wasted no time getting out their weapons; with Boomer having his boomerang ready to throw at the big guy, and Alan pulled out two pistols pointing them at the women.

"Stop!" Izanami shouted at them all.

The three guards stopped, before they all started fighting.

"This is a place of love, not war." She smiled, before turning her attention back to G.E.M.

"Don't look at me like that." She told him, "Your eyes don't scare me in the slightest."

"How about answering my question then?" He continued staring right at her, keeping his glare above eye level. It was tempting to leer down, but he fought against it.

"Okay." She leaned back in her chair. "To answer all your questions… Izanagi is dead."

"What?" G.E.M. asked her.

"You've been out of the loop for a while?" Izanami told him. "He has moved on to a new life. I have taken his place in this one."

"How?"

"I was his second in command." She pointed out to him. "You should remember that after all the times we spent together."

G.E.M. leaned back, getting a little red from her choice of words. Putting himself back together, G.E.M. got straight to the point. "I came here because there is something I need you to take off my hands."

"Why?" Izanami laid her elbows on the desk, and her head in her hands. "Is it hot?"

"Really hot." G.E.M. told her, "Scalding. Too hot for my crew and I to handle."

Izanami moved around in her chair, gesturing to him. "Sit down."

G.E.M. did as she asked, sitting across the desk from her.

"Tell me about it." She smiled, leaning in to listen.

"I can't tell you much about it," G.E.M. started explaining. "A few days back, we raided a ship." He stopped himself from telling her about it being a Valen ship. "Long story short, there was some top-secret items being carried on that ship directed for your territory."

"So, you stole Zǐ Sè Dēng Pào property?" Izanami started to stare him down now.

"No." G.E.M. quickly corrected her. "I 'stole' Hǔ Bǎi Hé property, and I need you to get it there, so I can get this heat off of us."

Izanami stayed silent for a few minutes, before responding to G.E.M.'s request. "What is this... thing you want me to take off your hands?"

"I honestly can't tell you." G.E.M. told her. "It is not out of any disrespect. I have all the respect for you and your crew, but you would not believe me if I told you."

"Try me." She said, leaning back in her chair, crossing her legs on top of the desk, and puffed her pipe.

"Okay, don't say I didn't warn you." G.E.M. paused to take a deep breath. "We have the Valen Princess, Zephyrus on our ship."

Izanami choked on her pipe, causing her to go into a choking fit. "You idiot!" She shouted, shooting up from her chair, and rushing to his side to grab him by the collar of his jacket. "You have done a lot of dumbass things in the past, but KIDNAPPING the Valen heiress? I should drag you out to the center of town and have all the crews take turns killing you! Do you have any idea the maelstrom you released on us with what you just did? No wonder Valen is attacking every pirate ship that they spot without mercy."

"We did not know she was on the ship! Let alone hiding in a chest!" G.E.M. shouted back at her. Grabbing her hands, he forced her to let him go. "If I did, I would have made sure she would not have been taken! Then she would have been dead!"

"What are you talking about?" Izanami questioned.

"If you have not learned, the Valen King is dead." He explained, "It's reported that it was natural, but we believe he could have been assassinated. Princess Zephyrus told us her royal adviser was planning a coup. She was being smuggled to your Kingdom for protection, but we messed things up."

"And now you unleashed Void on every pirate in the skies." Izanami crossed her arms.

"I know my crew and I have messed things up, but that is why we need you." G.E.M. told her, wiping off his shoulders and arms. "Look Izanami, your crew is the 'unofficial' armada of Hǔ Bǎi Hé.

You have pull with the government. I need you to take the Princess to your homeland, so she can be safe, and out of my hair."

Izanami paused for a bit, having to walk around as she thought it over. She would have been a sight to behold, if it was not for all the tension that filled the room. Her wooden sandals clicked across the floor with ever step.

She finally stopped, turning back towards G.E.M., saying, "Alright G.E.M., my bodyguards and I will follow you and your crew back to your ship. If what you are saying is true, we will take the Princess into our care, and get her to Hǔ Bǎi Hé. But!" She went right up to his face, "If you are lying about this, I will personally drag your sorry ass back to Valen, while dangling over the bottomless Void."

Chapter 21

"Damn!" Victor cursed, as he and Sunshine finally returned to the ship with their supplies.

Pinky walked over to them, having opened the docking bay door to let them in. "What's up?" She asked him.

"These parts cost me nearly an arm and a leg." He explained, "Ever single vendor jacked up the price of goods. I'm sure we are going to be losing money after we get rid of all we can sell."

"That is not going to be good for us." Pinky told him, sighing. She looked over at their loot from the raid, having divided the stuff they could sell from the stuff they could not sell.

"How have you guys been with protecting the ship… and the Princess?" Sunshine asked.

"So far it has been quiet." Pinky explained to them. "May is currently watching Princess Zephyrus in the kitchen and has made some soup for us."

"Leftover again?" Sunshine complained.

"Yes, again." Pinky said, facing him. "If you do not like it, you can starve or go out and buy yourself something to eat."

"Okay." Sunshine started to leave, before a quick check of his pockets made him realize he was flat broke. "Umm… Do you think I can borrow some money?"

"I don't know." Pinky told him, "With what Victor just told me, money might get a little tight around here."

Sunshine groaned, knowing Pinky was messing with him in the worse way. "Fine!" He gave in, "I'll have some soup." He stormed off, leaving Pinky and Victor alone.

Pinky watched Sunshine till he was out of sight and turned her attention to Victor. "How long do you think it will be till we can head back out into the skies?"

"With all the damage the ship has taken from the armada, the Red Chains, and the maelstrom," Victor thought it over, "I will be lucky if she is ready in a week."

"Well," Pinky shook her head at the news, "maybe we can use that time to rest up for a bit. I mean, we did nearly die three times."

"I just hope the Captain can convince Zǐ Sè Dēng Pào to take that troublemaker off our hands." Victor complained.

"I'm sure G.E.M. can do it." Pinky ensured him, "They are pretty close when it comes to all the crews."

"Okay then," Victor nodded, "I better get to work. The ship's not going to fix itself."

"Boy, it would be wonderful if it could." Pinky stated with a smile, as Victor headed off to get to work.

While that was going on, Princess Zephyrus was sitting in a chair, as May was stirring the soup to make sure it stayed warm.

"I'm bored." Zephyrus complained, swinging her legs to try, and fall, to entertain herself.

"I understand." May told her, as she finished stirring and placed a lid on the pot. She walked over to Zephyrus, sitting across from her. "We've been trapped in this ship for days. And now that we reached land, you have to stay here."

"I feel like I'm goanna go crazy." Zephyrus stated.

"Don't worry." May assured her. "Once the Zǐ Sè Dēng Pào take you under their care, you will not have to worry about being in this tiny tin can ever again." She chucked tapping the table top.

"Maybe you're right." Zephyrus agreed, before alarms started going off.

Alarms exploded with noise and caused the Green Coats to shoot to their feet. "What is that noise?" the Princess asked while holding her ears.

"We're under attack!" Pinky shouted to be heard over the alarms. "You go hide! Bob! Come with me!"

Pinky and Bob got to the hanger bay door just when it was forced open. The two watched as an orb was tossed and jumped to avoid an explosion, but instead of fire and shrapnel, it turned out to be a smoke bomb.

Pinky and Bob ducked behind some boxes, as the bullets started flying. There was no way they were going to be able to fire back with the smoke continuing to fill the hall. All they could do was sit there and wait.

Pinky waited, before noticing something coming through the smoke. It was the silhouette of man raising a sword over his head.

She used her gun to block the oncoming attack, getting a close look at their attacker.

He was an elegant looking man with clean, sun blond hair, deep sea blue eyes, and white skin. His clothing was just as elegant. She could only see his shirt, a pure white top with blue buttons, ropes, and shoulder pads

"Blue Bloods." Pinky growled, struggling to keep his sword away from her.

"Thanks for stopping by and getting all these treasures for us." He told her. "We'll be taking it from here now."

Screaming in rage, Pinky pushed him back into the smoke and started to fire.

It was quiet for a few seconds, before shots were fired right back at her, forcing her to dodge and roll.

Once the bullets stopped coming, she waited to see where the attacker was. The smoke slowly cleared to reveal Bob just standing there, pointing his gun at Pinky.

"Bob?" She questioned

"Pinky?" He said as well.

Pinky did not know what was happening, but she could see someone standing behind him. He was dressed just like the one that attacked her, but with chestnut brown hair.

The Blue Blood held his sword over his shoulder and beside his head, ready to strike down Bob.

"Bob! Look-" Pinky tried to warn him, but something knocked her on the back of head. She fell to the floor, her vision blurry, only able to see a fuzzy figure of Bob falling to the floor as well.

May was in the kitchen using a frying pan as a shield against one of the invading Blue Bloods that was attacking her with a cutlass. The narrow walk way was the only thing keeping the attacker from getting behind her.

The metal blade clashed with the underbelly of the pan, as May looked around for anything she could use to fight back.

A rolling pin came into May's view and she reached out for it. But that was not going to happen, as the attacker slammed his sword on the roll pin, cutting it in half.

With nothing left, May did the only thing she could think off. She got on her knees, put the cooking pan over her head, and begged, "Don't kill me."

Her attacker looked down at her. "Pathetic." He said out loud, before walking away.

May took her chance. Shooting up to her feet, she jumped, and swung the frying pan with all her might, hitting the Blue Blood on the side of the head.

The Blue Blood feel down onto the floor, and May felt excited, jumping in joy. That was until a pistol was pointing right in front of her face.

"Nice shot." They told her, "Now… Die-" He said but was cut off by something striking him in the back of the head.

May watched as he fell straight to the floor, revealing April right behind him, having thrown a scalpel at the Blue Blood.

"April!" May rushed over, hugging her big sister.

"You alright?" April asked her.

"Yeah, but what are we going to do about the rest?" May asked, worried.

"Follow me." April said, and the two got to work barricading the dining area door with anything that wasn't nailed down.

Victor was in the engine room with a wrench in his hand as a makeshift weapon and waiting for the invading party. A ding sound came, and Victor looked down to see a small ball bounced his way.

Victor took a moment to look at it, before the ball released a gas. Just one sniff of the gas caused, Victor to start feeling woozy and dizzy, before he fell to the floor and passed out.

As the knockout gas cleared, two Blue Bloods walked in with pistols and cutlasses pulled out. They looked around the area, only spotting Victor on the floor, before looking at the engine.

"Oh crap!" One of them declared, "Look at that thing!"

The engine was a mess. Duct tape covered about half of the wires and pipes, glass gages were either cracked or broken. The geo-sphere in the center of it all looked ready to explode any moment.

"We better just get out of here." The other said, "It was miracle these guys were able to make it through the Zone-X's storms."

"They must have a god looking out for them." The first said, before the two rushed out of the room, not wanting to tempt fate.

In Pinky's room, Princess Zephyrus hid under the bed, listening to the sounds of battle slowly going down. She hoped that meant that the Green Coats were winning, but that hope died when the door to the room swung open and revealed people who were not them.

She could see their boots made from the finest leather in all the Kingdoms, and fine, pure snow-white pants legs.

At least two men rushed in, looking around the area.

Zephyrus could feel her mouth about to move, but she covered it with both her hands.

"Is there anything here?" One of them spoke.

"Just your usual stuff." The other replied, "Nothing worth taking."

"Keep looking." The first said, "Don't leave anything unsearched."

Zephyrus just watched their feet moving around, as the sounds of drawers and closets opening could be heard. A realization came to her that they might just look under the bed and find her. She wished, she hoped, she prayed that did not happen, but as one of them walked over, they looked down and found her.

"Well, what do we have here?" They said, reaching out, grabbing her by her hair, and pulling her out from under the bed.

"Holy crap," The other stated when he saw Zephyrus. He was tall, with short pure blond hair and piercing blue eyes. "Who is this?"

"I'm not sure." The first one, with chestnut hair and eyes said, "But she has to be Valen by her clothing. And by that crest on her chest, clearly a noble."

"G.E.M. kidnapped someone?" The blonde started laughing.

Zephyrus tried to struggle and fight back, even being able to reach up and back hand the guy that was holding her in the face.

The slap caused him to lose his grip, and Zephyrus tried to escape, but the blonde grabbed her in his arms and lifted her into the air. "Got some fight in you?" He said, "I'm sure our Captain would love to know that there is another noble in town."

The chestnut guy rubbed his cheek as he said, "How are we going to get her out of here?"

"That's easy." The blonde said, "We just throw her in a chest."

Zephyrus was shocked by his words as she was carried off through the ship's halls to the cargo bay and thrown into an empty chest. The same chest she hid in when escaping her Kingdom.

Chapter 22

G.E.M. and Izanami walked back to the docks, side by side, with their crewmembers behind them. Most people looked on, watching the two captains walk by without a word.

G.E.M. did not know what Izanami was thinking as he gazed over at her along the way.

Everyone cleared a path for them knowing it was a horrible idea to get in the way of either captain.

A drunk man was wobbling his way towards them, with a bottle in his hand. He mumbled something under his foul breath, as he continued coming their way.

G.E.M. and Izanami stopped, waiting for the man to step aside, but he continued before bumping into both of them.

Before the drunk could say a word, Izanami stabbed him in the gut with the sharp end of her pipe. G.E.M. grabbed the man by the back of his shirt and pulled him off the pipe tossing him into the side of a building.

He pulled out his cutlass pistol and shot the man in his feet, kneecaps, and hip.

As the man fell to the floor, the two captains looked down at him. "I hope you live through this, so you will learn not to disrespect us with your drunkenness ever again." G.E.M. told him

"If you do live through this, it will be a good reminder for the rest of your life. But if you do, and stain my kimono with your filth again, you will not live to do it again." Izanami added in.

The group continued walking, till they started to see the docks. Looking over, they noticed smoke coming from there.

"Did a ship catch on fire?" Izanami pondered putting her hand over her eyes to see well. "I think that coming from dock-"

"My ship is stationed there!" G.E.M. panicked running at the smoke like a bat out of hell, with Boomer and Alan on his heels.

G.E.M. stared at his prized ship smoking when he reached the docks. "Oh no," he said, as they rushed into ship and shouting out, "Pinky!"

G.E.M. and the others called out for the rest of the Green Coats. "Pinky! Bob! May! April!" The smoke blocked his vision and filled his lungs. He coughed, trying to wave away the smoke as he kept searching.

It did not take long for him to find Pinky and Bob in the storage hall, both laying on the floor, passed out. Neither of them seemed to have any stabs, cuts, or bullet holes in them, so maybe they were okay.

"Captain!" Alan called out, causing him to turn and see him and Boomer had also run inside as well.

"Find the rest of the crew," He wasted no time ordering them, "and get them outside as quickly as possible."

Boomer and Alan nodded. Alan picked up his brother, putting Bob's right arm over his shoulder to carry him. "Come on bro, you're going to be alright." Boomer went deeper into the ship to the find the rest.

G.E.M. picked up Pinky bridal-style, feeling her weight in his arms as he carried her off the ship. There was a strange bump he could feel on the back of her head while carrying her. That must have been where she was hit.

Once they were off the ship, G.E.M. laid her on the ground and patted her cheek. "Come on. Wake up." He seemed to plead.

Pinky started groaning after a while, slowly starting to open her eyes.

"You are alive." G.E.M. said, "Good. Wait here, till the rest are out." G.E.M. did not give Pinky time to tell him anything, as he rushed back inside.

Luckily for him, Alan had already taken care of his brother, allowing him to join G.E.M. in their search for the others.

This time they covered their mouths, only breathing when it was necessary, and when they could find a pocket of clean air.

As they went down the hall, they saw Boomer rush past them, carrying a passed-out Victor on his back.

The two looked at each other for a moment, but that was wasting time. The hall was still full of smoke, so the two kept their hands on the walls to guide them and checked for doors, opening all the doors found along the way and banging their fists on those that were locked.

When they noticed the dining area door was locked, G.E.M. and Alan banged on it.

"May!" He shouted, banging on the door with his fist. "It's your Captain! Open up!"

"Captain?" May called out from the other side.

"Thank goodness you're here!" April's cry could be heard on the other side as well, causing G.E.M. to jump a bit. "Did you slaughter all those invaders?"

G.E.M. did not know how he should reply to that. He noticed Boomer running past them, understanding that they had this under control.

There was still Sunshine somewhere on the ship to save, and the Princess as well. Finally, G.E.M. responded. "They got away before we could get here. Open the door, so we can get you to safety."

It took them a while, but April and May were able to move aside their barricade and exit into the hall.

The four traveled down the hall, no one spoke, covering their mouths. April and May used napkins they had on hand, Alan used his clothing, and G.E.M. used his jacket cape. April hung on to G.E.M. like a magnet to iron, while May had her other hand on Alan's shoulder, following behind.

When they got out, G.E.M. saw Pinky helping Victor and Bob. Victor seemed perfectly fine for someone that was out cold a few moments ago. Bob was rubbing the back of his head, possibly from getting struck there like Pinky had been.

Looking over at April, G.E.M. told her, "Go help Pinky with the others. I'm going back to get you-know-who."

G.E.M. was ready to rush back in, but April continued to hold him. "What are you doing?"

"She is not there." She told him. "She was taken by the Blue Bloods."

"What?" He shouted.

"We heard them as they were coming through the hall." May jumped in, "They talked about how they found something 'really special' and how George would 'love to see this'."

G.E.M. could feel himself ready to panic. If they showed the entire island that the princess was with them, they would all be slaughtered, or worse pushed off the edge of the island into the Void.

G.E.M. pushed April off him and headed down the docks.

"Where are you going?" April asked him.

"I've going to inform Izanami what's happened." He told her. "It's the only way to keep us from getting killed right away." And with that, he left his crew to take care of themselves, while he went off to face Izanami once again to let her know the bad, no, worse news.

Chapter 23

Izanami reached the Green-Eyed Monster, watching G.E.M. and the two crewmates he had brought with him to meet her, rushing in and out to get the rest of the Green Coats out of their damaged ship.

"Should we help them Captain?" one of her bodyguards asked.

"You know the rules. A pirate crew's problem is not your problem." she told her guard.

"But what about… the 'package'?" the guard asked her.

Right at that moment, G.E.M. walked up to her clearly not happy about something. "The Blue Bloods attacked my ship." he told them, "They stole our bounty, including her."

Izanami eyes widened but soon narrowed. "How can I be sure that they have really taken her, when you have no proof that she was on your ship in the first place?"

"Are you god damn serious?" He shouted at her getting right in her face.

Izanami's bodyguards quickly defended their captain, attacking G.E.M.

G.E.M. jumped away, pulling out both S2BU and URF'D. "You are a real bitch. You know that?"

The female guard pulled out a katana, "We will teach you not to talk to our Captain in that manner."

The male guard pulled out his brass knuckles, cracking his knuckles as he slipped them on. "This is going to be better than punching up drunks."

"Are you going to have your crew fight for you?" G.E.M. asked Izanami ignoring the other two.

Izanami just stared at him, pulling her pipe out, before responding, "Do not kill him."

The guards and G.E.M. charged at each other ready to kill each other. The female guard swung first with her katana, which G.E.M. blocked with the S2BU.

He aimed the barrel of URF'D right at her face, but she was able to dodge by pulling her head aside right when he pulled the trigger.

G.E.M. did not have time to react to her, as the male guard punched him from behind, sending G.E.M. flying into boxes that were scattered on the dock.

Trying to recover quickly from being blindsided, G.E.M. turned over to face them, sitting back, and opened fire.

The woman dodged his shots with flips and twirls, while the man just sidestepped them like a professional boxer.

It only took five shots before both of G.E.M.'s guns were out of bullets. He cursed, "Shit!" when realize he had wasted six bullets on that damn drunk and missed the woman with the seventh. He did not have time to deal with that as the two rushed over to him.

Crawling back to his feet, G.E.M. positioned himself for their attack, but before they collided,

238

something swirled between the three forcing them
to stop.

The three watched as it spun around two
guards and returned to Boomer who caught his
boomerang easily.

Everyone on the docks watched as Boomer
walked up to his captain and smacked him right
across the face with the back of his hand.

G.E.M. held his cheek and yelled at
Boomer, "Why the hell did you do that?"

Boomer replied by bopping him on the head
and pointing over to where rest of the crew was.

G.E.M. realized that Boomer was telling
him that there were more important things to worry
about at the moment than the fight that was
happening.

G.E.M. looked over at Izanami and her
guards, "If you want to kill me, you will have to
wait. I've got to get back at the Blue Bloods for
attacking my crew and save our 'prize'. If you want
to follow us, then don't fall behind."

Izanami and her guards were dumb founded as they watched G.E.M. rush over to his crew, asking them, "How is everyone doing?" G.E.M. asked.

Pinky looked up at her Captain, addressing him first. "We are going to be okay."

"How many of you are strong enough to fight?" he asked.

Boomer gave a thumb up, and Alan responded with "I'm perfectly fine. I want payback for Bob." G.E.M. knew they were good; they were with him during the attack anyway.

May said, "I'm good." Victor said, "I'm a little woozy, but I'll be fine." Sunshine said, "Same"

"You three should stay back." G.E.M. told them, knowing they were not really fighters.

"No!" May shouted, "They got-" G.E.M. was sure she was going to say 'her', but thankfully April covered her mouth before that could happen.

The stares of the gathering crowd were causing G.E.M. to become uneasy, wondering if they would try to go after the Blue Bloods as well as the valuable 'treasure' they had just lost.

"You're going to need me to get in." Sunshine spoke out, "I'm the best hacker there is."

"And I want revenge for what they did to my baby!" Victor shouted.

G.E.M. did not want to keep fighting with them. Time was of the essence.

"I'm more than ready to cut them open." April declared, "I want to see if their blood is really blue."

There was no argument from G.E.M. She was highly skilled with those scalpels; even beyond just for surgery.

Bob and Pinky seemed to be a little bruised, but they looked ready to get revenge on the Blue Bloods.

"If Alan's going!" Bob declared, "I'm going as well."

Pinky looked right at her captain. "I guess we're all going to the Blue Bloods."

"Then get up!" He ordered, "We got to catch up with the Blue Bloods, and make sure our 'treasure' is safe!"

Realizing he said it out loud, G.E.M. looked around at the other pirates that perked up at the word 'treasure'.

"I suggest you all erase those thoughts from your minds!" He shouted, reaching into his coat pockets to reload his guns. "Or I will erase them for you!"

The other pirates quickly lowered their heads, not even daring to look at G.E.M. for fear of death.

"All of you come on!" He waved his crew, before starting to walk off. "We're wasting time!"

The entire Green Coat crew got up and follows their captain to get back Princess Zephyrus, and some payback.

Chapter 24

The Green Coats marched through the streets shoulder to shoulder with a desire for revenge and a thirst for payback.

Every single one of the Coats carried their weapons open for all to see and get out of the way. G.E.M. had both his S2BU and YRF'D gripped tightly in his hands, ready and loaded. If he gripped any harder, he would unwittingly pull the triggers.

Alan, Bob, and Pinky had all their guns ready to support their captain.

May had brought along a frying pan.

Boomer had his trademarked boomerang. April had some scalpels gripped between her fingers. Victor brought the biggest wrench he had. Sunshine had some gadget with him.

Everyone that saw them coming, got out of their way. All it took was one look into G.E.M.'s monstrous, green eyes, and the people would step aside.

As the group continued, the streets started changing. The streets were cleaner, the houses were finer and better kept, iron gate fences surrounded a few of the houses, and men in armor came marching towards them, carrying spears like walking sticks.

"Halt!" One of the men ordered, pointing his spear at them.

G.E.M. was about ready to shoot the guy, but Pinky beat him to the punch and shot the man.

The other man watched his friend drop dead, before turning towards the Coats to possibly attack them. This was quickly erased from his mind, when seeing five guns, a boomerang, scalpels, and frying pan all aimed at him.

Being outnumbered, the man dropped the spear and was about to run away.

"Hold it right there?" G.E.M. commanded. "Where is the Lord George?"

"Lord George?" The man asked, his armor rattling.

"The only one that controls the entire Blue Blood armada." G.E.M. pointed out.

"I heard gun fire over here!" A voice came from behind them.

"Someone's been shot!" Another voice came from their side.

Soon a large number of guards surround them, pointing their spears at the Coats

The Green Coats quickly formed a circle to watch each other's' backs, as spearmen surround them from all sides.

The guard still standing readied, his spear once again pointing it right at G.E.M.'s bare chest.

"You want to see Lord George so badly?" The guard told him, "Then we will take you to him... as our prisoners. Now... hand over your weapons!" He ordered.

G.E.M. wished he could blow his brains out for giving him orders, but he didn't want him and his crew to end up as Green Coat kebabs. So, with no other ideas that would not ending up killing them, G.E.M. reluctantly handed STBU and URF'D to him.

He looked at the rest of his crew, gesturing with his head for them to do the same.

They did, some more willing than others.

"Now," the guard said, getting behind him, before ordering and poking him in the back. "Start moving!"

G.E.M. jumped and hissed. The spear head had poked his injured spot. He gave the guard a 'I'm going to remember that' look, before moving down the street.

The rest of the crew followed, all with spears behind their backs.

"Put your hands up!" The guard ordered. "I want to make sure you don't try anything funny."

"Believe me," G.E.M. told him, putting his hands in the air. "I'm all about being serious."

With that, the Blue Blood's guards were leading them down the road.

As they continued down the streets, the houses got bigger and larger. It seemed there was no end to the mansions, with some of the properties being at least a block long.

Luckily, G.E.M. and the others were finally reaching their destination. At the end of the road was a massive set of gates that connected to walls so high, not even all the Green Coats could get over it if they tried to standing on each other's shoulders. They could not even see the house down the endless driveway.

It would almost seem like they would have to walk, but a carriage was in view, as the gates slowly started opening for them.

"Get in." The guard ordered, forcing the entire crew to cram together inside the carriage.

As they rode off, the Green Coats talked amongst themselves. "What do you think is awaiting us?" Pinky asked.

"I don't know," G.E.M. told her, "but I don't like it."

"What's so bad about the Blue Bloods?" Alan asked.

"Besides the fact they attacked our ship, stole our stuff, and now we are being carried to them as their prisoners?" Bob added in.

"Do I need to spell it out for you?" He shouted at the twins. "They are some of the worst pirates in the skies. Worse than the Red Chains. They think their better than everyone else, and can steal from whoever they want, just because they are from 'noble' blood."

"So, what are we going to do when we meet Lord George?" May asked.

"I could cut him up for you." April suggested.

G.E.M. looked at her with a mixture of fright and a desire to let her cut loose. "Let's see what happens." He told her.

Sunshine sat quietly, trying to look out of the carriage the best he could.

Boomer just sat in the middle quietly, staring out into nowhere.

As they got closer, they could finally see the manor, or mansion, coming up. It looked more like a five-star hotel than a house.

There were at least five floors and it was a mile wide. There were five front doors, each leading to a different area inside.

As they rode around, they could see the pearl, sparking white clean walls, the golden frame windows, and the blue curtains inside.

Maids, butlers, and other servants walked around, working or carrying trays.

The crew looked out in confusion. Of course, there would be servants going around, but they were rushing around like headless chickens.

They got their answer, when they were taken to the back, and saw a massive party being held.

They could hear musicians playing smooth, soothing music. White and blue tables, chairs, and pathways spread around the garden. Everyone was dressed in suits and dresses.

The carriage stopped, and the Green Coats were forced out by spear point.

G.E.M. took the lead, keeping his hands over his head, as the rest of the crew slowly followed behind him.

Everyone at the party stopped what they were doing and turned to stare at the Green Coats being escorted.

"Well, isn't this a pleasant surprise!" One voice shouted.

The Green Coat looked out, as one man came strolling up to them.

He was in his late twenties, 30 at most. He was dress like an admiral in a white suit with blue shoulder pads and epaulette. He had blond neck length hair tied in a short pony tail. His face was square shaped, with a chin that could chop wood.

When he came up to the Green Coats, he greeted, "Welcome honor guests slash prisoners. To my garden party."

Chapter 25

The Green Coats looked at their "host", with spears surrounding them on all sides ready to strike.

G.E.M.'s green eyes narrowed on Lord George. His beautiful bleach blonde hair, his shiny unblemished skin, his perfectly pressed uniform. It made G.E.M. want to throw up and break him in two, preferably not in that order.

"It's been a long time," He started to say, but as he opened his mouth to finish, G.E.M. interrupted him.

"Don't you dare say that name!" He shouted, getting several spears coming right up to his face.

"Captain!" His crew cried out, worried for him.

Lord George just looked at him, smirking without a care. "Put away those spears." He ordered the guards.

"Aw?" They all looked at him like he was crazy.

"But sir…" One of the guards asked.

251

"They are not just my prisoners… but also my 'guests'." He told them. "It will be alright."

The guards followed his orders, slowly backing away and lowering their spears.

G.E.M. was ready to kill Lord George, when he heard a familiar annoying voice called out. "Pinky!"

Cutting through the crowd, looking no worse than when she was taken, was the Princess Zephyrus.

She rushed over to them, weaving and squeezing her way through everyone. When she got close, Lord George cut off her path by placing his arm in front of her.

She pushed it aside to get through, but he grabbed her by the back of her dress and threw her behind him. "Keep her there." He ordered.

The guards replied, "Yes sir," and pointed their spears at her.

Pinky started in shock, and G.E.M. just stared like a mad dog and charged at Lord George.

Lord George turned back to see G.E.M. ready to kill him with a punch to the face, but just dodged and delivered a knee to G.E.M.'s injured stomach.

G.E.M. felt all the air escape him, falling to his knees, and grabbed his gut. He felt his bandages getting wet and knew his wound had been reopened.

"That's a pretty bad injury you got there... b- I mean G.E.M." Lord George said, standing over him. "It was stupid of you to try and attack me like that with a gut wound."

Lord George walked in front of G.E.M., looking down at him as only his kind would do to G.E.M.'s. "I heard the rumors that *you* killed the Valen princess. But low and behold, you have done something even worse. You brought her to our secret island."

"We had no choice!" Pinky told him.

"Really?" Lord George asked her. "And you thought bringing her to an island full of the most dangerous pirates in the world was a good idea?"

"It… was… our only… option…" G.E.M. replied, struggling to speak from the pain.

Lord George looked down at him, smirking. "Well, if that's the case. How about you all stay and celebrate with us?"

"Celebrate?" May asked.

"For what?" April added.

"For us capturing the Valen Princess, and the traitorous pirates that brought her here." He said, smirking. With a snap of his fingers, the guards surround them once again.

"Yes sir?" They awaited his orders.

"Bring them up to the main table." He ordered, "It would be nice for them to enjoy one last meal, before they die."

"No." The Princess shouted, reaching out to them, but the guards continued blocking her path.

"Don't worry." Lord George told her. "You'll be joining them."

The Green Coats were escorted through the crowd. G.E.M. had to be lifted and dragged by two guards, still feeling his wound bleeding.

His crew noticed this and spoke up. "We have to help him." Victor told them. "Please."

"Why?" Lord George asked, leading the group. "When you're all about to die anyway?"

As they got closer, they looked around at the other party guests whispering and chatting among themselves.

As they started to reached the table, they were all shocked at the sight of a gallows right behind it.

"That's just decoration." Lord George joked, "Nothing to worry about."

'Translation, you're going to die.' G.E.M. thought to himself, looking up at the nooses swaying in the breeze.

Princess Zephyrus and the Green Coats were set at the main table, being offered fancy dishes of finger foods and wine. Nobody ate anything but just looked up at the crowd staring at them like animals in a zoo.

"What's wrong?" Lord George asked, taking a cracker with cheese and meat on it, and tossing it into his mouth. "Not hungry."

"No…" G.E.M. groaned in pain.

"No, you're not hungry? Or no, you are hungry?" Lord George messed with him.

G.E.M. groaned at him, this time in anger.

As the party seemed to be going on, Pinky leaned over to G.E.M. to whisper, "What are we going to do Captain?"

"I'm thinking." He told her, wishing he had an idea that would save their necks, before they found themselves hanging from them.

Lord George turned to his other guests, spreading his arms wide with immense joy. "Friends, colleagues, honored guests." He looked over at the Green Coats with a knowing smirk on the last line, before turning his attention back to the crowd. "I have a great show for you today! We are going to be punishing the traitors that brought an outsider to our island."

The crowd booed, and possibly would have thrown food at them if it wasn't impolite.

"Now, now," Lord George tried to calm them, lowering his hands. "That's why we have the gallows. We haven't had a good hanging in a long time. As a matter of fact, I think this is my first time. Right G.E.M.?"

G.E.M. looked up at Lord George, still holding his injured stomach. The look on Lord George perfectly pretty face had G.E.M. just wanting to put a bullet into each of his eyeballs.

That was it. "A duel!" G.E.M. cried out with all the strength he could, getting the attention of the entire party.

Lord George looked right at him, confused. "A what?" He questioned.

G.E.M. slammed his hand on the table, struggling to get to his feet. His crew reached out to him, worried for his wellbeing. "I challenge you… to a duel. If I win… You let us go…"

Lord George cupped his chin, thinking it over. "I don't think so." He told him. "Why should I?"

"Because your honor as the Blue Bloods' captain will be in question if you don't accept." G.E.M. explained to him, forcing a tiny smirk on his face.

The party goers start mumbling, talking, and gossiping among themselves.

"Alright, you got your duel." Lord George agreed, "It will be more fun to kill you myself anyway, G.E.M."

"Not if I kill you first." G.E.M. told him.

Chapter 26

Two butlers dressed in white and blue walked up to the table the Green Coats were sitting. Both had pillows in their arms. The one on their left had a pair of pistols, and the other had a pair of rapiers.

"Well, Captain G.E.M." Lord George spoked in a smug tone. "Choose your weapon, and we shall duel with them."

G.E.M. only needed a moment before pointing over at the butler on the left and said, "Pistols."

"Very well." Lord George said, walking over to the pistols and picking one up.

G.E.M. struggled to get up, groaning and holding his stomach, causing his crew to rush to his aid.

"Captain!" They cried out.

Pinky was the first to grab him, making sure he did not fall over. "Don't do this. Have one of us do it."

"Yeah," Alan said, having to be the second crew member to help hold him up. "Have Bob or I take over."

"Yeah! I'm a way better shot than Alan." Bob said, getting a dirty look from Alan.

"No." He told them, getting himself straighten out. "I have to do it. I issued the challenge, so I've got to take it."

With that, he made his way around the table to the butler holding the other pistol. He picked it up, examining it, then looked over at Lord George with questionable eyes.

Lord George looked back. "Is something wrong?" Lord George asked him.

There was a lot wrong, but G.E.M. did not want to hear Lord George's lies and excuses. "No." He said, starting off their duel with a stare down.

With a shrug, Lord George replied, "Fine then. Let us get started."

The two were led to the middle of the walkway nearly shoulder to shoulder. G.E.M.

looked over at Lord George's smile, wanting to shoot those pearly whites out of his mouth.

Once they reached the spot, G.E.M. and Lord George stood back-to-back, facing opposite directions.

A different butler from the other two came up to them. "Gentlemen. As you… should know, you will both take ten paces, before turning and opening fire. Is that understood?"

"Yes." G.E.M. answered.

"Of course." Lord George replied.

"Then you may begin." The butler told them, stepping back.

G.E.M. and Lord George started walking, their steps being counted out loud by the butler. "One! Two!"

G.E.M. could not shake the feeling that something was up with this duel.

"Three! Four!"

He felt Lord George was going to shoot him in the back, or possibly have some guards ready to shoot him from all sides.

"Five! Six!"

G.E.M. looked closer at the pistol. As far as he could tell nothing was wrong with it, but it did not feel right.

"Seven! Eight!"

Something was wrong with the pistol, but how was he going to win without pulling the trigger?

"Nine!" The butler dragged it out.

'Well,' G.E.M. thought, 'best to wait and see.'

"Ten!" The butler shouted, and Lord George turned around and fired. G.E.M. dodged the bullet, having ducked and rolled the moment the butler finished counting.

The bullet flew overhead, and G.E.M. stopped on his back, aiming the pistol at Lord George. "You just wasted your one shot." He bragged.

Lord George was shocked, looking down at G.E.M. aiming the pistol at him, but he soon smiled. "It seems I have." He said, dropping the pistol to the ground, and putting his hand over his head. "Go ahead and take your free kill."

"Sure." G.E.M. said, getting back to his feet. "But I want this to be very personal." He walked over to Lord George, seeing his smile slowly turning upside down.

As they stood face to face, G.E.M. put the pistol right between Lord George's eyes. "I wish I had two, so I could shoot both your eyes out, but I guess between the eyes will have to do. Unless... you have something, you'd like to say?"

Lord George stared down the barrel and looked over to see G.E.M.'s finger slowly starting to pull on the trigger.

"Okay! Okay!" Lord George shouted. "The gun is set to explode when the trigger is pulled!"

G.E.M. let go of the trigger, pulled it away from Lord George's face, and twirled it in his hand. "I knew something was up. You always were a cheat."

The Green Coats and the princess cheered for Captain G.E.M. They started rushing over to them, when the guards pointed their spears at them.

"Hey!" G.E.M. shouted, looking over at his crew being blocked off. As he turned back to Lord George, he found a sword pointed right at his neck.

"So, what if I was cheating?" Lord George told him. "You still didn't pull the trigger. Therefore, it is a draw, and you, your traitorous crew, and the Princess will all hang."

G.E.M. glared at Lord George, as guards came over, grabbing him by the shoulder, and dragged him off to the gallows with the rest of his crew.

They were forced up the steps and lined up. The guards made sure to tie their hands behind their backs to keep them from fighting back.

"Please tell us you have a plan." Pinky looked over at her captain.

"You must have one." April responded, looking over Pinky's shoulder.

"Winning was my plan." He told them, looking over at his crew. "And I didn't win."

"I'm going to miss you bro." Bob told his brother.

"We're both going to die." Alan tried to insure him.

"Yeah, but you're going to be stuck in the Void, falling forever." Bob said, "But me, I'm going to be with mama in the sky beyond. I'll be sure to give her a hug and kiss for you when I get there."

Boomer stonily stood there with his chest pumped out and head held high. If there was any fear, he hid it under his mask and poise.

"I'm going to miss my ship." Victor said.

"I never got to cook a grand feast." May said.

Princess Zephyrus looked out at the crowd. Tears streamed from her face as she thought about how she failed her grandfather. She was about to hang, to die, and Yan was going to get the throne.

Lord George walked up to the gallows, enjoying the sight like it was an art piece. "It's going to be fun watching you hang b-"

"I am not who you think I am!" G.E.M. cut him off once again. One final act of defiance before he died.

Lord George shrugged his shoulder. "Whatever. Pull the leveler!" He ordered.

The one chosen for the executioner gripped the leveler in his hands. Before he could pull it however, something flew over the heads of the princess and the Green Coats, cutting all the ropes in one go. It struck the wooden pole, revealing it was a shuriken.

A cloud of smoke appeared at the top gallows hanging beam, clearing to show Izanami standing there.

"Am I too late for the party!" She called out to everyone below.

"Izanami!" Lord George shouted in shock, "What are you doing here?"

Izanami smiled down at Lord George. "I came here for the Princess, and the Green Coats."

"Well, you can't have them. Guards!" Lord George ordered, but huge plumes of smoke started appearing all over the place.

The smoke cleared and the Baron, his guards, and his guests were surround by ninjas with their swords drawn and ready to strike all who got in their way.

"I would think twice, before you decide to turn the entire Zǐ Sè Dēng Pào armada your enemy now, wouldn't you?" Izanami smugly asked him, crossing her arms over her chest.

Lord George glared at Izanami with the blades close to his neck. A smirk appeared on his lips. "Alright," He said, before drawing the sword at his side and cutting the ninja down.

"I thought you would do that." Izanami told him, "So I brought these." She pulled out the Green Coats weapons and toss it to them.

G.E.M. and the other quickly freed themselves, before jumping off the gallows into battle.

Chapter 27

As they landed on the ground, Alan and Bob opened fire on the crowd. The partygoers either ran for their lives or grabbed their weapons to join in the fight.

The two brothers made their way thru the crowd, watching each other's back by standing back-to-back.

Guards charged from Alan's side. "Here they come!" Alan warned.

They wrapped their arms together, with Alan bending forward and picking Bob up. Aiming at the charging guards, the two opened fire on them, hitting each one dead on.

Once that was done, Alan set Bob down. They quickly looked at each other, before shooting behind the other's head to take out another enemy.

"Lift me!" Bob told his brother.

Alan gave Bob a boost, and soon Bob was standing on Alan's shoulders. Forming a human tower, the two laid down cover fire for the Zǐ Sè Dēng Pào and their fellow crewmates.

If one ran out of ammo, the other would just cover them till their brother could reload.

"Ah!" The screams of a guard came towards them from behind.

Hearing him, Bob jumped off Alan's shoulders, performing a back flip that allowed him to take the guard down before he could get close.

"Nice shot bro." Alan told him.

"Thanks." Bob responded, "What should we do now?"

"Get the Void out of here, what else do you think we should do?" Alan said.

"I was thinking we go inside the mansion and see about stealing as much of our treasure back, and their treasure for good measure."

Alan nodded in agreement, as they rushed for the mansion.

Boomer tossed his boomerang from the gallows, before jumping down. Slowly making his way through the party, he reached up and caught his weapon coming back to him.

Decapitated bodies littered the grass, all victims of his whirling blade of death. A survivor came charging at him from the left with his sword drawn.

Boomer did not even look towards the attacker, as he stepped back enough for the Blue Blood to miss him.

With the Blue Blood bend over, Boomer kneed him in the gut, while dropping his elbow onto their back. The Blue Blood's eyes popped, as he screamed to high heaven, before dropping to the ground.

Boomer just looked at him for a moment, before stepping on his back and continued onward.

Party goers that were frozen behind and under their tables watched at the most mysterious member of the Green Coats made his way past them. They prayed to their gods that he would not notice them.

Boomer stopped and turned his head towards them in a flash. Fear gripped them all in a tightening hold that slowly sucked the air out of them.

There was no way to read Boomer's face through the full head mask he wore. No words came out of his mouth, if he could speak, or had a mouth for that matter. They all felt the grim reaper standing behind, ready to take their souls.

But that did not happen, as Boomer turn his head back and continued walking.

Five guards came towards Boomer, with their spears pointing right at him ready to strike. But they were all fools, and soon to be dead fools, as Boomer tossed his boomerang once again.

In one fell swipe, all five guards were dead, more victims to Boomer and his boomerang.

With little else to do, Boomer just continued on his way through the fight.

Chapter 28

The ladies of the Green Coats put up a strong fight as well. April and May acted stealthier, only attacking when they were either spotted or get a quick hit in.

They were both hiding behind one of the fallen tables, peaking over slightly to look for a path.

"I found two of them!" A guard shouted, causing them to turn and see him pointing over at them.

April throw one of her scalpels, striking the guard in the right eye.

He screamed, dropping his weapons to pull the blade out.

This allowed May the chance to rush over and swing her frying pan, knocking him out.

"Come on." April said, grabbing May's hand and pulling her along.

"Where are we going?" May asked her.

"We're going to find that blue bastard and make him pay for hurting G.E.M." April told her, "Only I get to do that."

"But what about the others?" May asked.

April hid them behind another flipped table, before pointed over to Boomer cutting down his latest unfortune opponent. April then spotted Alan and Bob going into the mansion, possibly to steal as much stuff as they could carry. "I think they can take care of themselves." She told May.

"Forget I asked." May said.

They spotted a guard looking around but not seeing them.

April looked at May. "Stay here." She told her.

Sneaking out from behind the table, April slowly made her way to the guard. In a quick flash, April covered his mouth with one hand and slit his throat with her blade in the other.

"April!" May called out. April looked back, only to find her held hostage by a Blue Blood.

April was about to attack. "Na ah ah," the Blue Blood said, holding a pistol to May's head. "One more step, and this lovely young lady gets it."

"I'm sorry April." May apologized, "I was so focused on you, that I didn't see him."

April's anger caused her to grit her teeth. "What do you want?"

"Well…" The Blue Blood thought, "I think I want your sister to come with me and be my… woman. I think that's the best way to put it."

"You'll regret it." April warned him.

"By you?" The Blue Blood laughed. "I highly doubt it."

April looked over at her sister. "Don't be afraid. You can get out of this."

"How?" May cried.

"Yes sis, how?" The Blue Blood said.

"You got your great weapon on you. It's in your hands." April told her.

He looked down at the frying pan. This caused the Blue Blood to laugh, but May knew April was right.

With a mighty swing upwards, May smashed the pan into the still laughing Blue Blood's face, before lowered the pan, and broking the Blue Blood's nose. Red blood dripping out of it. His face looked like something out of a cartoon, as his grip loosened, and he passed out onto the ground.

"Good job." April told her. "Now, let's find G.E.M." She took May's hand again, and they rushed off.

Pinky took Princess Zephyrus by the hand, leading her through the panic, with her pistol in the other. As they were running, the sound of gun fire nearby made them duck behind a flipped table.

Pinky hugged the princess close to her, keeping her back to the table as an extra layer of protection. In case that was not enough.

"Nice work dodging that." A voice spoke out. "How about you come out from behind there and let me try again?"

Pinky opened her eyes, slowly letting go of the princess.

"If not," The voice continued, and Pinky realized it was a woman's voice. "I'll just come over there."

Pinky was kneeling, while the princess laid on the grass behind table. "What are we going to do?" Zephyrus asked.

Pinky did not want to risk poking her head out and getting a bullet in return. "I don't entirely know." She said, "But I have to try something."

She poked the barrel of her gun over the table and fire a single shot.

There were a few moments of silences, besides the rest of the fighting and panic going on, before the woman on the other side responded.

"Were you hoping to randomly hit like that?" She said, before shooting and hitting the table.

"Aa!" Pinky shouted, grabbing her left shoulder.

"Sounds like I hit something." They said, "That means I get another shot."

Pinky quickly got down, covering Zephyrus, as another bullet flew through the table and over their heads.

"Guess I didn't get anything that time."

Pinky looked down at Zephyrus. "Stay here." She whispered, before getting back to her knees.

She knew she only had one shot at this, or she would die. Pushing out with all the strength in her legs, Pinky launched herself from the table.

There stood her target. A woman wearing an what appeared to be a large, white powdered wig, and a large, poufy white and blue dress. Her make-up made her look like a clown.

She did not have time to compare beauty tips, as Pinky drove across the ground, pointed her gun right at the woman, and fired.

The woman did not have time to react, as the bullet hit her right in the stomach, knocking her down.

Pinky landed on the ground with a thump. Luckily landing on her good shoulder.

"Pinky!" Zephyrus shouted, rushing over.

"I'm fine." Pinky said, getting up. "Let's find the others and get you out of here."

Chapter 29

Victor and Sunshine were far from the fighting types, so they spend the entire time weaving around the area.

They found themselves in the mansion. "What are we going to do?" Sunshine asked.

"Let's see if we can steal one of those carriages and some horses so we can get the Void out of here!" Victor explained.

Finding the horses was easy enough, as they were all in the stables. The horses were jumping around in their pens, neighing in fear.

Victor could not get close enough to them. "This is impossible." He spoke.

Sunshine touched him on the shoulder. "Allow me." Sunshine said.

He slowly went up to one of the horses, holding his hands out. "Easy there." He softly spoke, slowly waving his hands up and down. "Easy."

Victor did not know what to expect as Sunshine got closer to it. Once he was close, the horse seemed to calm down, and Sunshine was petting it. "There we go." He told the horse, before looking over at Victor. "Let's get that carriage."

That part turned out to be harder said than done. With everyone running around like headless chickens, and the guards fighting, there was no one guarding the carriages.

"Which one should we take." Sunshine asked, holding the horse by the reins.

"That one." Victor pointed to one that was big enough for all of them, but light enough for the horse. "Come on."

The two wasted no time. As Sunshine kept the horse still, Victor went to work hooking it in. It was surprising easy for him, as he seemed to do it all in under a minute.

Victor hopped on first, offering his hand to Sunshine. "Come on!" He shouted. Sunshine took it and was pulled up. "Let's get the Void out of here!" They cracked the reins and rode off to find the rest of their crewmates.

G.E.M. and Izanami fought against George together. Their blades clashing with one another the entire time.

Despite being two on one, George's sword skills allowed him to block every attempt the two made to stab or slash at him.

"Is this all you two can do?" Lord George mocked them.

"No." G.E.M. told him. "I can still do this." He pulled the trigger on his cutlass pistol but missed.

Izanami tried to stab him in the liver, but George blocked the attack, pushing it away from his body.

"I think it's my turn now." He said, going on the offensive.

G.E.M. and Izanami flipped and spun around to avoid his attacks, making his attacks just as useless.

There seemed to be no end to this duel. "What are we going to do?" G.E.M. asked Izanami, dodging another attack.

"I'm not sure." She replied, side stepping an oncoming attack.

"You could just die." Lord George suggested, still swinging at them.

As the fight continued, G.E.M. glazed at George's feet and got an idea. "Izanami!" He called, getting as close to her as possible to whisper the rest. "Get him to hold still for five seconds. I'll take care of the rest."

"What?" Izanami questioned, but G.E.M. was already gone, and she ducked to avoid George nearly taking her head off.

She did not know what G.E.M. was planning, but it was better than jumping around.

Lord George brought his sword up over his head to cut her down. She saw her opening and thrust her bladed pipe forward and up into George's right arm.

He screamed and groaned, stopping in his tracks.

There was his moment. G.E.M. aimed both his weapons and shot Lord George right in the feet.

Lord George lost his footing and fell to his knees. His sword fell out of his hand and got stuck in the ground behind him.

G.E.M. walked up to George, pointing the barrels of his guns right at George's eyes. The blades making two small cuts into underneath. "Now…" G.E.M. told him. "You are going to allow us to leave here safe and sound."

"Why would I do that?" Lord George told him.

G.E.M. just cocked the hammers of his pistols, ready to fire.

"Okay. Okay." Lord George said, "You win. You and your crew are free to go."

"And the Princess?" Izanami added.

"And the Princess."

"We will also be taking back the treasure you stole from us, as well as anything else we can carry." G.E.M. said.

"What?" Lord George looked up in shocked.

"To the victor goes the spoils." G.E.M. said. "Or should I take your life as well, Georgy?"

George growled. "Alright. Just go."

With the princess safe, and their treasure back and then some, the Green Coat and the Zĭ Sè Dēng Pào rode off with the carriage and the horse that was now theirs.

Chapter 30

G.E.M., Princess Zephyrus, and Izanami
were all back in Izanami's office quarters in her
brothel. Everyone else was ordered to wait outside
the office, as the three of them discussed what had
happened over the past few days.

"And that's when I met G.E.M. and his
Green Coats." Princess Zephyrus finished
explaining her story.

Izanami nodded, sitting back in her chair
with her feet on her desk. "I see." She said, "I am
sorry about your loss. But it seems good fortune
smiled on you when G.E.M.'s men took you. If they
hadn't, you would have surely been dead by now, or
at the very least a prisoner in your home."

"And you know about the Valen armada
nearly blasting us out of the sky, the Red Chains
nearly butchering us, and you were there when the
Blue Bloods nearly hanged us." G.E.M. added.

"And the gods cursed me by having *you*
survive all of that." Izanami coldly insulted him.

"What can I say? I'm the best there is in the skies." He proudly boasted, leaning back into his chair with his hands behind his head and closing his eyes.

Izanami and the princess just stared at him for a moment, before looking at each other and shaking their hanging heads.

Opening one of his eyes to get a peek at what they were doing, he straightens himself back up. "So," G.E.M. firmly asked her, "will you take her with you, back to your country, and help her get sanctuary?"

Izanami leaned on her desk, crossing her fingers in front of G.E.M. and the Princess. "I will help escort the Princess to Hǔ Bǎi Hé, but you have to come with us."

"Wait? What?" G.E.M. cried out. He shot out of his chair, slamming his hands on the desk. "You can't be serious!"

"But I am." She said, leaning back into her chair with a crooked smile

Just then, the door burst opened. Both Zǐ Sè Dēng Pào and Green Coasts rushed in. "Is there something wrong?" They all shouted at the same time.

"Nothing's wrong." Izanami told them. "Please go back outside."

Her men bowed, starting to leave. The Green Coats looked at their captain, and he just nodded, telling them, "You heard her, wait outside."

Once everyone was out, and the doors were closed again, G.E.M. and Izanami turned to talk to each other again. The princess sat there. Her eyes swinging back and forth between the two.

"Okay, why do you want us to come with you?" G.E.M. asked her.

Izanami got up. "It's simple." She said, "You want to prove you're innocent? You bring the Princess with you, we escort her safely to meet with the Emperor, and we all leave happy."

"Do we have to take him with us?" Princess Zephyrus asked her.

"And what if I refuse?" G.E.M. asked, crossing his arms.

Izanami started making her way around the table. "I'll answer your question first G.E.M." She said, getting in close.

G.E.M. watched her, wondering what she was planning. His eyes followed her, as she rested her hand on his, slowly rubbing it.

"The answer," Izanami said, "is quite simple." Before G.E.M. could react, Izanami grabbed him by the wrist and covered his mouth with his own hand, pressing hers against it. While he was focused on that, she let go of the first hand, took her pipe, and shoved the bowl end into his injured area. "If you don't do this, I will personally make sure Lord George hangs you high for the world to see. You will not be able to escape me. Not in my house. Not on Teach Island. Not even if you hide out in one of the Seven Kingdoms."

G.E.M. groaned in pain, as the bowl dug deeper.

Izanami looked over at the princess, who was clearly frighten by her action, she gave her a pleasant smile. "And yes dear," She sweetly said, "we do need him. It's his fault we're all in this mess, and I want to make sure he fully cleans it up."

Pulling her pipe away from G.E.M.'s ribs, she jumped on her desk, taking a seat, and making sure to cross her legs.

G.E.M. coughed and gasped to catch his breath, before looking up at Izanami right in her face. "You are one crazy woman."

"Maybe," Izanami said, shrugging it off. "So, do we have a deal?"

G.E.M. and Princess Zephyrus looked at each other, then back to her. "Fine." He agreed. "Take us to Hŭ Băi Hé."

Special Thanks

Aunt Tana

Ron and Beth Kennon (my mother and father)

The rest of my family

My friends

McKendree Writers

O'Fallon's Writing Group

And you for your support